Also by Gail Gilchriest

The Cowgirl Companion

Bubbas & Beaus

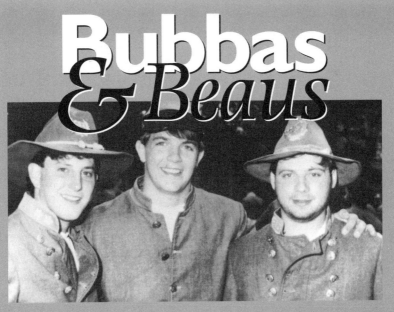

FROM GOOD OLD BOYS TO SOUTHERN GENTLEMEN,
A CLOSE LOOK AT THE CUSTOMS, CUISINE,
AND CULTURE OF SOUTHERN MEN

GAIL GILCHRIEST

HYPERION

New York

Library of Congress Cataloging-in-Publication Data

Gilchriest, Gail
    Bubbas & beaus : from good old boys to southern gentlemen, a close look at the customs, cuisine, and culture of southern men / by Gail Gilchriest
        p. cm.
    ISBN 0-7868-8055-4
    1. Southern States—Social life and customs—1865– —Humor. 2. Men—Southern States—Humor. I. Title. II. Title: Bubbas and beaus.
    F216.2.G55   1995
    975'.04—dc20   94-23699
                                                                      CIP

First Edition
10 9 8 7 6 5 4 3 2 1

DESIGN/PRODUCTION BY ROBERT BULL DESIGN

For
G.W.G., E.W.G., and G.B.G.,
three fine and funny Southern Gentlemen

CONTENTS

ACKNOWLEDGMENTS

Every now and then you meet a character, one of those individuals about whom everybody says, "Somebody should write a book about him." My friend Chrissy's daddy is one of those guys. Somebody should write a book about him, and in a way, I have.

That's where my research started at any rate, with George Armstrong. Chrissy took a break from her job on Wall Street to help. After a quick stop in New Orleans to have our fortunes told, she and I headed to Natchez to bask in her daddy's gentlemanly Southernness for a few days. George was a good starting point. Talking to him before embarking on a book about Southern men was like studying the owner's manual before attempting to operate a new appliance. George introduced us to his friends, to his dog, to his friends' dogs. With him, we walked through cemeteries, ate good food, and wallowed in some mighty high-quality visitation.

When Chrissy's vacation time ran out, my friend Sophie joined me. She went to college in North Carolina and has a passel of friends scattered around the South. We headed straight for the bluesy part of the Delta—Clarksdale, Mississippi—the birthplace of Muddy Waters, B.B. King, and our friend Mahlon Bouldin. From Mahlon's we went on to Alabama, and then to Atlanta, and Charleston, and Chapel Hill, and Memphis. Taking our time, we looked up friends and friends of friends along the way.

In Georgia one night, we sat around in a hamburger joint talking with some guys Sophie knew from school. "Southern men, huh? What will you do for your research?" one of the boys wanted to know.

"I'm doing it right now," I confessed. Once they understood they were being studied, my subjects became less talkative. But still, we had a great time—there and all around Dixieland.

As I continued to gather information, my friends kept saying "I can't believe that shooting the breeze with Southerners is really your job!"

I couldn't believe it either. What good fortune to have such colorful and righteous subject matter. Seems to me that Southern men, along with fat people, represent the last bastions of socially acceptable prejudice. They sure take plenty of heat in the media. During the past few decades Dixie boys have been caricatured as wife-beating racist illiterates. I envisioned correcting this popular misconception as a part of my mission. I'm not saying there aren't some bad guys down South; there are. But to my way of thinking, the good guys far outnumber the bad. The bad ones just seem to hog the spotlight. When one Southern gentleman learned of my project he asked, "Are we finally coming back in style?" It's about time.

I'm not attempting scholarship here. This isn't rocket science, or even sociology. Once in a while I've taken the liberty of embellishment; in other spots, I've thoroughly disguised identities so as not to hurt any feelings. The names throughout the book have been omitted to protect the unaware and the publicity shy.

Special thanks to all the Southern beaus and belles who spoke with me, especially to:

George Armstrong, Fred Parker, Dora Clark, Bobby Scudamore, Judy and Larry Tarleton, Julianna and Alfred Pinckney, John Elderkin, Bobby Tucker, Randy Farmer, Kit Sharp, Carrie Pepi, Al Grovemyer, David Kaplan, Karla and Jim Man, Pam Francis, Nancy Chapman, Kathy Lendech at Turner Entertainment, John White at the University of North Carolina, Elsa Cook of the Gloucester *Gazette-Journal* in Virginia, Sharon Sarthou at the University of Mississippi, Major Rick Mill at The Citadel, Hamilton and Rosalie Horton, Ray Talley, Elizabeth Rape, Dr. Mel Bouldin, Marshall Bouldin, Mahlon Bouldin, Dean Zachary, Betsy Moye, subscribers to the Southern Cultures electronic bulletin board, Julia Shivers and John Boles at *The Journal of Southern History*, John Shelton Reed, all the gifted storytellers in my hometown of Silsbee, Texas, my friend and excellent editor Sophie Sartain, fact-checker Michael Casella, old friend Jackie Golden and her family, Chrissy Armstrong, Cynthia Kinney, Jane Rucker, David Thompson, Lauri Nelson, my mom, Shirley Gilchriest, Christy Archibald, Mary Ann Naples, Laurie Chittenden, Lauren Marino, and especially to my agent Geri Thoma for getting me going on Dixie boys in the first place.

Painting with a Big Brush

Two Words: Rhett and Ashley

I'VE BEEN THINKING ABOUT MEN LATELY, MORE than usual, and in a more scientific way. Especially Southern men. You know the ones. Those pretty boys liable to talk as slow as molasses, and behave bolder than a steaming cup of chicory coffee, and to look cooler than a long, tall drink of water whenever they go sashaying by in their natty seersucker suits. I've been thinking, and I believe I've finally figured them out.

Seems to me that two words tell the whole story. That's right. Total insight into Southern masculinity can be found in two simple little words. Now, if you guessed "red" and "neck" you'd be close, but wrong. "Chicken" and "fried" is a commendable shot, but no bull's-eye. Give up? The alpha and the omega of Dixie manhood, right here: Rhett and Ashley. The rascal and the gentleman.

Think about it. Down South when a girl's not being helped on with her wrap by a courtly Ashley type, she's probably being hit on by a dashing Rhett clone. And very occasionally, if she gets plumb lucky, she

---

A BRIEF HISTORY OF SOUTHERN MANHOOD

Southern men didn't just scramble out of the primordial ooze in their four-by-four pickup trucks and start drinking beer and shooting squirrel right away. Oh, no, there's been a whole lot of evolving going on in Dixie in order for indigenous manhood to ascend to this current, sublime state of grace.
(This time line will continue down here throughout the book.)

40 B.C.   Greeks begin Southern custom of clay-eating.

might win the jackpot and be dealt a fellow possessing the more desirable attributes of both.

Oh, how Scarlett loved that Ashley Wilkes! If you'll remember, even when he went off and wed sniveling Miss Melanie, Scarlett continued to carry a mighty flame for the hand-kissing master of Twelve Oaks. Meanwhile, Rhett Butler hankered, in the most manly way, after Scarlett from the get-go. But she'd have none of it. Her heart belonged to Ashley right until the day she finally got a whiff of the coffee, at long last realizing that he had never harbored any smoldering passion for her after all. By then poor Scarlett had cooked her goose but good with Rhett. Or had she?

THE FRONT PORCH:
Gone With the Wind

AT MORE THAN 25 million copies worldwide, Gone With the Wind *holds a place somewhere between* Quotations from Chairman Mao *and* The Valley of the Dolls *on a list of the best-selling books of all time. The film has been seen by more individuals than the total population of the United States. Go anywhere in the world. Mention the American South. People will think of* Gone With the Wind. *It's as Southern as the Southern belle, Southern hospitality, or Southern fried chicken.*

Almost fifty years after its publication, it continues to do brisk business. All thanks to Margaret Mitchell, "the little lady of the big book." Drawing heavily upon Southern stereotypes, Mitchell's fiction fermented the long-simmering myth of the Old South. The result: an overnight literary sensation. David O. Selznick bought the film rights for $50,000. When the movie premiered in Atlanta in 1939, the entire city shut down for three days of parades and balls. Following the hoopla, the demure author took ill in grand Southern-belle fashion. Mitchell's husband diagnosed the vapors afflicting his wife as the "result of becoming too famous too suddenly."

Today in Atlanta, the Road to Tara Museum celebrates the city's Gone With the Wind *identity. The exhibits in the museum are not devoted to Atlanta's Old South history. Nor do they pay homage to the enduring literary depiction of a lost way of life. Instead, The Road to Tara honors the picture show based on the book about the Old South—a movie filmed entirely in Hollywood.*

A BRIEF HISTORY OF SOUTHERN MANHOOD, continues

Either way, Margaret Mitchell sure did hit upon a big truth when she dreamed up Rhett and Ashley. Those two embody the dilemma so many of us, especially Southern belles, face when browsing the man market: Do I board life's predictable merry-go-round with a steady-as-she-goes Ashley by my side? Or do I priss myself right out and gamble on a ticket for the roller coaster, climb into the last car with Rhett, and throw my hands in the air as we whip around the curves?

Flesh-and-blood versions of those *Gone With the Wind* leading men thrive in the New South. The only difference is, today Rhett and Ashley are commonly known by more generic terms—the Good Old Boy and the Southern Gentleman. Like the beret-wearing French *boulevardier* or the mustachioed Italian *bon vivant*, the Southern Gentleman and the Good Old Boy have emerged as trademark phenomena, our mascots, unique symbols of a colorful region—one an Ashley, one a Rhett, both possessing a certain rakish charisma that neophytes would do well to study before setting a dainty foot below the Mason-Dixon.

Any Southern girl can sniff out the difference between the Gentleman and the Good Old Boy, nothing to it. The Gentleman enjoys opera. The Good Old Boy likes wrestling. The Gentleman pulls trout from a babbling brook with fly tackle, while the Good Old Boy shocks catfish out of the bayou using dynamite or an old crank telephone.

The Southern Gentleman speaks softly, slowly. He wears custom–tailored seersucker suits. He worships his ancestors, adores his children, and heaps thoughtful trinkets and adoration upon his wife *and* his mama. He reads, he gardens, he hunts, and he strictly adheres to the rituals of the civilized, daily cocktail hour.

Then there's the Good Old Boy. He reminds you that there's a dang sight more to being Southern and male than drawling "yes, ma'am," quoting Faulkner, and mixing up a dandy julep. All that dashing-beau stuff represents only half the story. There's the whole back-slapping thing too. Good-old-boy can be a verb, you know. And in some areas of the South, an unsuspecting person of the Yankee persuasion risks being good-old-boy'd to death.

Instead of lacing up white buck oxfords, the Good Old Boy pulls on Red

101 USES FOR KUDZU
#7—Villain in a Japanese monster movie.

Wing work boots. He wiggles into denim rather than seersucker. He's heard of Faulkner all right, but he probably quotes more often from the collected works of Lewis Grizzard. And girl, when that five o'clock whistle blows, don't look to find the Good Old Boy mixing a pitcher of mint juleps on the verandah. No, ma'am. He'll more likely be popping open a can of Dixie at the local juke joint or sitting sunk down in the truck sucking on a bottle of Jack Daniel's wrapped in a brown paper bag.

Sometimes you can tell a Southern Gentleman from a Good Old Boy by his name. The Gentleman gets christened

RHETT. . . ASHLEY. . .

Bill Clinton	Al Gore
Clarence Thomas	Thurgood Marshall
Terry Bradshaw	Arthur Ashe
Billy Carter	Jimmy Carter
Sam Walton	Colonel Sanders
Burt Reynolds	Gregory Peck
Goober	Howard Sprague
Jesse Helms	Sam Nunn
Charles Barkley	Michael Jordan
Boss Hogg	Robert E. Lee
Foghorn Leghorn	Pepe LePeu
Jimmy Johnson	Tom Landry
Tom Sawyer	Forrest Gump

A BRIEF HISTORY OF SOUTHERN MANHOOD, continues

1607   Indians serve grits to settlers in Jamestown.

DEFINING DIXIE

EVEN THOSE WHO warm to the old Confederate geographical boundaries have a tough time arguing regional uniformity. No longer just a lush land of feudal plantations, racism, and bootleg whiskey stills, the South today boasts almost as much diversity as, say, Western Europe. Geography, history, and identity have gotten so knotted up together below the Mason-Dixon that many outsiders just give up and go home rather than try to untangle the miasma of the several different regional psyches.

Take the short course.

Virginia and North Carolina, along with parts of South Carolina and Georgia, constitute the Colonial South. People in those areas fancy themselves as Rebels, all right, two-timers; once they rose up against England and won, then they picked a fight with the Yankees and lost. Given a choice between a lingering psychological alliance with a winning cause or a losing one, they've opted for the obvious.

Denizens of the Deep South—the farmlands of Mississippi, Louisiana, Alabama, Tennessee, and the eastern parts of Arkansas and Texas—lack the luxury of being able to decide which history to highlight. They've simply taken an inglorious heritage and made it magnificent.

A third region of the post–Civil War South defies clear categorization. It's the Fringe South—Florida, the western parts of Arkansas and Texas, parts of Kentucky, and West Virginia (and even the Washington, D.C., suburbs of Virginia). When the Stars and Bars flew, those freshly annexed territories were toddlers still. At that crucial moment in history when the more mature Southern states were so galvanized by secession, the junior members of the Confederacy had yet to establish strong regional personalities. And then there's the hills.

Almost as much as race divides Southern society, a more subtle imaginary line separates highlanders from lowlanders. The low-country people—those living along the Gulf and Atlantic coasts as well as in the Delta—have long viewed themselves as aristocrats, gentleman farmers, feudal lords. The highlanders— folks who settled in the mountains of Tennessee, Kentucky, Georgia, Alabama, and the Carolinas—have traditionally worked as industrialists, miners, craftsmen. For generations, the hillbillies have played Irish or Scottish to the planters' British. But fact is, even though the land puts on a change of clothes near the Ozarks, Smokies, and Appalachians, the hill-dwellers and the flat-landers have both been smelling the same magnolia for generations. Today much more unites them culturally than separates them.

One Southern Gentleman born in flat Mississippi and now living in rolling Tennessee summed it up this way: "It's the difference between Memphis and Nashville, blues and bluegrass; one's about the Delta, the other's about the hills."

something dignified, pompous–sounding like "Hamilton Charles Davis Fitzhugh IV," while the Good Old Boy goes by "Billy Wayne, Jr." or "Jim Buddy." The Gentleman answers to the nickname "Four" or "Ham." The Good Old Boy says "Huh?" whenever someone hollers "Hey, T-Bone!" or "Looky here, Big 'Un!"

If you look further, you'll notice that the Good Old Boy/Gentleman distinction ignores bloodlines. Consider the case of the Carter brothers of Georgia—Jimmy and Billy. A picture of little brother Billy, for example, would be appropriate alongside a dictionary definition of Good Old Boy, even though big bro Jimmy qualifies as a hall-of-fame Southern Gent.

The difference doesn't spring from economic status either. Wal-Mart billionaire Sam Walton prided himself on his Good Old Boyishness, while chicken tycoon Colonel Harland Sanders walked the walk and talked the talk of an authentic Southern Gentleman.

Education and intellect don't figure much into the equation. Take Senators Sam Nunn of Georgia and Jesse Helms of North Carolina as a case in point. Two smart, well-educated guys in the same job, yet one's a Gentleman, the other Good Old Boy to the bone.

And there's no racial discrimination involved. White quarterback and Louisiana native Terry Bradshaw swaggers through life a textbook Good Old Boy. Arthur Ashe, the late tennis legend from Virginia, exemplified Gentleman both on and off the court. Clarence Thomas? A belly-scratching Good Old Boy, of course. But Thurgood Marshall? Eternally the Gentleman.

There are sloppy-speaking boneheads among us who believe that Good Old Boy and Bubba can be used as interchangeable terms. Well, not so fast. A girl might tree a Bubba or two in Biloxi, but Good Old Boys don't do Boston. They are indigenous to the land of cotton. Think of the Good

BUMPER STICKER

AMERICAN BY BIRTH.
SOUTHERN BY THE GRACE OF GOD.

Old Boy as a superior Southern subspecies of Bubba. Bubbas may well form the backbone of the nation, but Good Old Boys make the South stand straight and tall.

Looking around, I've noticed that we've got a complete line of Good Old Boys down here from which to choose—the Basic Good Old Boy, the Redneck, and plain old Trash. Some say the difference has to do with breeding. Others suggest it's attitude. One Cajun Good Old Boy explained the distinction as "a certain gin nay say quah." Humorist Roy Blount, Jr., once noted that "Good Old Boy" means approximately the same thing as "mensch." Billy Carter—an authority on the subject if ever there was one—described the Good Old Boy as a guy who drives around in a pickup drinking beer, depositing his empties in a sack. A true Redneck, on the other hand, tosses his empties out the window, while Trash builds a pyramid with them in his living room and calls it "art."

I like to break it down this way: The Basic Good Old Boy raises live-

IF WE CAN PUT A MAN ON THE MOON . . .

GIVEN THE CHOICE, which name would the modern belle like to see at the top of her dance card—Rhett or Ashley?

"Rhett," says an artist in her early thirties. "Who'd want that whimpering Ashley?"

The second woman questioned, that's who. And the third. "For a life mate or for a roll in the hay?" the third woman, a financier with Mississippi roots, wanted to know. "Because for a life mate, I'd choose Ashley—more stable. But for fun—it'd be Rhett all the way."

Not all belles made the call so quickly and decisively. "Would Rhett love me the way he loved Scarlett?" one woman asked. "If he would I'd choose Rhett in a New York minute. If he wouldn't, I'd have to go with Ashley. I mean, in a loveless marriage you might as well hook up with a nice guy, huh?"

"Ashley didn't have a good sense of humor," one belle pointed out, "and sense of humor is key for a Southern girl."

An older woman, married, divorced, and thinking about retirement, wanted neither Ashley nor Rhett. She said she'd already tried both types more times than she cared to count. "You know who appeals to me most at this point in my life?—Mammy."

A BRIEF HISTORY OF SOUTHERN MANHOOD, continues

FIVE SURE WAYS TO TELL
IF YOU'RE IN DIXIE

1. You are in a state that is frequently mentioned in country music lyrics.
2. Complete strangers ask, "How's your mama and them?"
3. There are more "Dixie" listings than "American" listings in the telephone directory's business pages.
4. *Southern Living* and *Guns & Ammo* are the only magazines in the doctor's waiting room.
5. You ask people if they're Southern and they say, "Hell, yeah!"

stock to sell. The Redneck raises livestock to eat. Trash raises livestock to date. The Basic Good Old Boy spits tobacco juice into a brass spittoon. The Redneck spits into a Coke can. Trash, too broke to spring for a pouch of Bull Durham, chews toothpicks or matchsticks. The Good Old Boy plays politics. The Redneck plays football. Trash played the banjo in *Deliverance.* You get the general idea.

Now, Gentleman covers a wide spectrum too—seems to me we have the Refined Gentleman, the Dixie Poet, and the Classic Mama's Boy. Here the difference has little to do with breeding or attitude and everything in the world to do with the specific nature of a man's neurotic obsession.

The Refined Gentleman cares most about heritage, history, and civility. The Dixie Poet cares about academics, storytelling, and Faulkner. The Mama's Boy cares about getting home in time to drive his favorite girl to the beauty shop for a wash 'n' set. The Refined Gentleman flunked out of Washington and Lee. The Dixie Poet teaches at Mississippi State. The Mama's Boy studies dental hygiene at the community college down the street. The Refined Gentleman re-creates his past to make it seem more aristocratic. The Dixie Poet rewrites his personal history to make it seem more gothic. The Mama's Boy gallantly lies about *his* age when Mama gets a face-lift.

Southerners call this rather politically incorrect stereotyping "painting with a big brush." I'll admit, it has its limits. The pigeonholing game gets a little dicey when you throw in all the pretenders. The South bulges with Gentlemen affecting the Good Old Boy shuffle and with upwardly mobile Good Old Boys, or "yuppabillies," trying to pass themselves off as Gents. But that's Southern schizophrenia; things really get crazy when Yankees try to shuck and jive like authentic Dixie men.

Shoot, most of those Northern boys might as well go ahead and wear "kick-me" signs on their backs as try to fake Southern-fried sex appeal.

The great thing about this kind of name-calling is that Good Old Boy need not be a negative, and Gentleman rarely rates as out-and-out flattery. The old image of the Good Old Boy as a wife-beating, racist illiterate with tobacco juice running down his chin galls the renaissance Redneck. At the same time, the modern Southern Gentleman can't seem to shake the old sissy label fast enough either. That "hint of mint" dogs him wherever he goes.

For all their differences, the Good Old Boy and Gentleman share quite a few traits. Neither hesitates to play the chivalry card—opening doors, tipping hats, and pulling out a chair before a girl's feet even get tired. Both support their families, try to do right by God, and like to have a good time every now and then. Both are loyal. Both love ladies, like liquor, and hold quality bullshit in highest regard. Both have a weight problem—one's always too fat, the other perpetually too skinny—and both ignore it. They agree that pound-for-pound, Junior Samples is fun-

A TOUR OF BEULAHLAND

Good Old Boy	Southern Gentleman
• Christ of the Ozarks	• Sewanee
• Dollywood	• Colonial Williamsburg
• Graceland	• Monticello
• The Educated Animal Zoo	• The High Museum
—Hot Springs, Arkansas	• Churchill Downs
• The Raceway at Darlington	• Crook's Corner
• South of the Border	—Chapel Hill, North Carolina
—North Carolina/South Carolina state line	• Sea Island, Georgia
• Grand Isle, Louisiana	• Appomattox
• Rock City	• Houston Grand Opera
• Grand Ole Opry	

A BRIEF HISTORY OF SOUTHERN MANHOOD, continues

nier than Howard Stern, and both would rather watch an Andy Griffith rerun for the tenth time than tune in a brand-new episode of *Murphy Brown.*

Whether you've snagged yourself a Southern Gentleman or snuggled up to a genuine Dixie Good Old Boy, you can bet he'll grip his sides and beg for mercy whenever he hears a joke involving a talking dog, flatulence, or the man from Pawtucket. Unless he happens to hear such a bawdy tale from the lips of a woman. Then he's guaranteed to excuse himself, politely, PDQ.

Gentleman or Good Old Boy, the Southern man wants the world to know he's Southern above all else. He's devised a thousand ways to assert his regional identity instantaneously, no pussyfooting around. Upon meeting someone new, he stretches those vowels out a little longer than usual and rejects the letter r altogether. His slouch becomes more casually confident. He slaps some extra spit and polish on his already sparkling manners and shifts the old flirt engine down into overdrive. For the Dixie boy, flirting is like snoring; he's not even aware he's doing it.

Yet as much as he adores women, he could hardly be called a feminist. Instead, he's a masculinist. He draws serious, big-time pleasure from man's stuff—a bass rig, a shoe shine, a haircut, new tires, a complete set of socket wrenches. Those things make him happy, make him growl, make him feel even more like himself. He doesn't necessarily oppose equal rights for women. It's the difference between the sexes, not the inequity, that appeals to him.

"I'm a member of three all-male clubs," one Southern Gentleman told me proudly. "You might say I'm a radical masculinist."

That masculinism can be attractive. When you consider it for a minute, who makes a better mate for a feminist than a masculinist? Hey, modern women are coming back to real men, and the South is the real man's most natural habitat. Some gals prefer Good Old Boys, and others swoon for Gents. As Southern folks say, "It takes all kinds to make a world—and isn't that a shame?"

Even former radical liberal Jane Fonda (many Southern men's idea of the Antichrist) married herself a Dixie boy this time around. Old Hanoi Jane has said that her new husband Ted Turner knows better than some of the outdated "woman's place" ideas he holds, but can't help himself. He was raised that way.

Sure, Southern men can be obnoxious. Crude? Sometimes. Infuriating? Usually. But hey, they're sweet-smelling, friendly, brave, and mostly honest. Manly? Yeah. Sexy? Hell yeah, even the ugly ones. Whether they're black or white, macho or sissy, bone thin or a little on the chunky side, Dixie boys bring something special to the game. They combine the wisdom of Solomon with the strength of Hercules and the good looks of Samson—or at least Burt Reynolds. Southern men are big, bold, gaudy, top-of-the-line. Built for comfort, not speed—they are the Cadillacs of males.

Skeptical? Go to Washington. There you'll find a pair of Beulah boys running the show. While Bill's and Al's agendas may not be strictly Southern, their political styles certainly are. The Capitol currently qualifies as a Southern city again, now that Bill Clinton and his friend Al Gore have hit town. The Sabbath sunrise usually finds Bill and Al warbling "Amazing Grace" and enjoying a little fire-and-brimstone over at the local Baptist church.

Bill and Al prove the theorem too. One's a Rhett, the other an Ashley. You don't really need me to tell you which is which.

CHAPTER ONE

The Husk Right Off the Corn

"How's About You 'n' Me?"

A MIDWESTERN BOY MIGHT FANTASIZE ABOUT marrying a woman with big breasts. A Yankee man may long to settle down with a girl who earned herself a Phi Beta Kappa key. But the Southerner dreams of marrying a belle who's worn a crown, any crown. Once hitched, he'll treat her like a queen for life.

First prize would be a reigning Miss America fresh off the runway from Atlantic City, but competition for those gals gets fierce. For the average Southern guy, a former Miss Alabama wouldn't be anything to sneeze at, or even a Memphis State Homecoming Queen, Miss Stock Car Racing, or Miss Georgia Redneck. A woman who's reigned over even the dinkiest debutante cotillion rates as a quality catch. A prom queen runner-up, a princess, or just a lowly duchess counts as a better score than showing up at the altar with no royalty at all. About the only type of queen the Dixie boy wouldn't consider as a bride would be a New Orleans drag queen, and even then he'd take a gander in the direction of the scepter just to be sure.

Southern males seem to work up quite a lather when it comes to beauty pageants. The head judge at the Miss Arkansas pageant traditionally dresses up in a hog suit and squeals out his choice for the top prize. For the Miss Mississippi contest, one fellow on the panel wears a tuxedo made from Confederate flags. They call this region "the Pageant Belt." The name fits too, since girl-watching rates up there near stock-car racing as the Southern man's favorite spectator sport. Just as the race fan fantasizes about leading Dale Earnhardt's pit crew, the male pageant groupie hopes someday to present six dozen roses to Miss USA and then of course to marry her.

Since there are seldom enough certified, card-carrying beauty queens to go around, Southern boys just go ahead and treat most every woman as if she'd just won the swimsuit competition or aced the talent segment by playing "Dixie" on the spoons. Southern mothers deserve the thanks for this deluxe treatment. It's like belle karma: Southern mamas raise their boys up right, mannerly and respectful of women, so they'll make good mates for some other gal down the line. When it comes to romance and hot-monkey love, Southern men simply can't be beat. Why else would Scarlett have endured being lashed into that torturous corset?

In an age of phone sex, personal ads, and computer dating, the sweet-talking Southerner sometimes seems like an anachronism, but he's far from obsolete. He and his buddies have constructed quite an elaborate pedestal for their feminine ideal to occupy. The dynamic of

THE FRONT PORCH:
Moonlight 'n' Magnolia

*T*O *FIND authentic moonlight 'n' magnolia romance in your local bookstore, look for a paperback with gold-embossed lettering on the front. The title might be* Babes in Beulahland *or* Dixie's Daughter *or* Wild Stead of South Oaks. *Readers hot for tales of lust in the Old South should search out the work of Frank Yerby. Connoisseurs of soft-core Southern fiction consider him the inventor of the entire genre. Picking up where Margaret Mitchell left off, Yerby may not have introduced sex to the South, but he practically single-handedly familiarized the rest of the world with the steamy, euphemistic nature of Dixieland romance.*

Most Southern men had rather hunt in panty hose than read a Frank Yerby novel. Although you'd never in a million years get a Dixie Boy to admit it, he'd probably enjoy all the heaving bosoms and languid surrenders as much as he would looking at the pictures in a girlie magazine.

Why? Because at the same time women wish Southern men could be more like the pulp-fiction hero—bold, passionate, in touch with his feelings—Southern men dream of a woman in the Scarlett tradition—beautiful, high-strung, and, unlike the "easy" girls he sees naked in Penthouse, *hot only for him.*

A BRIEF HISTORY OF SOUTHERN MANHOOD, continues

Southern courtship involves the man waiting patiently for the lady to tumble off the platform he has placed her upon, while the woman frantically tries to maintain her tenuous balance up in the clouds.

Sex ranks high on the Dixie boy's top-ten list, but he enjoys the company of women even when he's standing up and fully clothed. Southern men don't generally fancy androgynous, fashion-model gals. Instead they go bird-dogging after women who look like women—big hair, curvy figures, layers of makeup, and no shoulder pads, please. A guy in Mississippi tells what he calls "a real sad story" about his girl cousin who went off to Harvard and came home awfully smart, but with all traces of her Southern belle erased. "She quit wearing lipstick, let the hair on her legs grow out, and started cooking tofu burgers out on the grill for all the world to see."

Southern men often say that the most effective form of birth control is a Bronx accent. A Dallas boy who moved North complained to his mama that there were no good-looking girls to date in Yankeeland. To support his case, he pointed out that Vermont had never placed a woman in the Miss America finals. He knew why: "They don't fix up. I don't think they bathe regular. And I guess nobody has told them that they're supposed to blond their hair and spray it up pretty."

Down below the Mason-Dixon, the mating season reels on a loop and has no end. Just under the surface of everyday Southern life slips an expectancy, a sense that something is fixing to happen—something big, something sexy. Somebody, somewhere is about to pop, to scream, to reach a quivering climax. Beulahland boys feel this tension and keep their fingers crossed: "Please, God, let that somebody somewhere be me."

Certified charm machines, Dixie men flirt year round with the ardor of stags at the height of the rut. Quentin Crisp, a British author and traveler in the South, noticed that Southerners "would like for you to want something, so they can give it to you." True, the Southern man would like for women to want something in particular—sex—so he can gallantly oblige.

Keeping this in mind, I've noticed that there are two basic approaches the Southern man takes to flirting. There's the familiar "Goober" method and

101 USES FOR KUDZU

#39—Name for a rock 'n' roll band.

TON

A BRIEF HISTORY OF SOUTHERN MANHOOD, continues

MIXED MARRIAGES

Ted Turner and Jane Fonda
(Georgia)   (California)

Victoria Reggie and Ted Kennedy
(Louisiana)   (Massachusetts)

Bill Clinton and Hillary Rodham Clinton
(Arkansas)   (Illinois)

Marla Maples and Donald Trump
(Georgia)   (New York)

Kim Basinger and Alec Baldwin
(Georgia)   (New York)

Frank Gifford and Kathie Lee Gifford
(Texas)   (Maryland)

James Carville and Mary Matalin
(Louisiana)   (Illinois)

Paul Simon and Edie Brickell
(New York)   (Texas)

Al Gore and Tipper Gore
(Tennessee)   (Washington, D.C.)

the slightly more esoteric "Cary Grant" way. Any woman with Southern experience will probably recognize both.

Named in honor of the service-station attendant in Mayberry, the Goober method goes something like this: If he's hot for you, Goober sneaks up behind you and claps his hands over your eyes. "Guess who?" More than likely annoyed, you play along and ask, "Who?" Your desire is pretty basic—you want an answer, plain and simple. And after a few whining "Guess, c'mon, just guess" teases, he'll give you what you want—"It's me, Goober! Heh, heh!"—feeling quite pleased with himself.

Less sophisticated uses of this same

technique might involve telling knock-knock jokes rapid fire or making rude-sounding noises with his armpit. The real rustic might ask you to pull his finger, or he'll do that little Three Stooges trick where he gets you to look down and then he makes a Curly sound as he flutters his hand in front of your nose, and says "Gotcha!—heh, heh!" In these instances you eventually demand that the guy stop pestering you. Thus Goober sets up the sitch: The woman wants something, the man delivers.

Along with Gregory Peck, Cary Grant still rates way up there on the Southern woman's male-order wish list. The mating dance, as choreographed in the Cary Grant school, works this way: A Southern Gentleman approaches and feigns indifference toward you just long enough for you to become interested. If you smoke, he'll make a big show of sucking pure pleasure from a cigarette. If you look thirsty, he'll elegantly swish the olive in his martini. After dangling the bait a bit, he'll begin to reel you in with "You surely do look parched. Would you like for me to get you some punch?" You would. He fetches it. Your hero.

Now it'd be tidy to assume that Good Old Boys always try to catch girls with Goober-esque charm and that tuxedo-clad Southern Gentlemen always drop a line with Cary Grant suave. Often it happens that way, but not without exception. That's precisely what makes Southern men such complex beasts. Each one of them mixes various ratios of Goober to Cary Grant. The trick for the Southern woman comes in deciding exactly what combination floats her boat.

ONE DIXIE BOY'S
HONEYMOON HORROR STORY

FLYING RICE hit my wife in the eye as we left the reception, broke one of her contact lenses. Then, on the way to the hotel late that night, she started hollering for me to pull over so she could go to the bathroom— she was about half drunk, I think. Anyway, when she got back in the car, she'd been bitten all over her feet by fire ants—they'd gotten in her panty hose or girdle or whatever. Next morning she had herself a killer hangover, and her feet were so swollen she couldn't even get her shoes on. Then, on our first day at the beach, she got so sunburned that she couldn't leave the room for the rest of the trip. Lucky for me I met this guy named Steve. He was on his honeymoon too. His wife had the flu. He and I went deep-sea fishing nearly every day. Had a fine time. He's the one you see in most all my honeymoon photos.

A BRIEF HISTORY OF SOUTHERN MANHOOD, continues

She has to think fast because flies seldom have time to settle on the Southern rake. He's all nerve and no nerves. After being sentenced to twenty-four years in the hoosegow for armed robbery, one Southern romeo asked the female prosecutor who'd arranged his trip up the river: "Honey, would you want to go out with me when I get out of jail?"

Like an animal with impeded night vision, the Southern man on the prowl is unable to discern between indifference and a come-on. To him, absence of outright rejection equals success. "She didn't slap me, so I asked her out."

One Southern Gentleman remembered the moment he first met his wife, thirty-plus years ago. "I screwed up all my courage and squeaked, 'Hey' as she passed me by at a pool party. She said 'hey' back, so about a week later I asked her if she'd like to go get a Coke. That went okay, so I married her."

Between "hey" and "I do" much palm sweating and backseat necking usually transpire. Down South, boys and girls still date. He calls for her at the assigned hour, ringing the doorbell with a box of chocolates or a corsage in hand. He endures an excruciating visit with her daddy while she squirts more mousse into her hair. Then, before delivering the belle safely home again, the Dixie boy dutifully tries to get into her pants. He fully expects to be unsuccessful, but for him it's as much a part of the romance ritual as splashing on the Aqua Velva.

When a Southern girl dabs Evening in Paris on her pulse points, pulls on her white gloves, or fastens her push-up bra, she's likely off for a night of heavy drinking at the country club with a gentleman wrapped up pretty in his tuxedo and duck-print cummerbund. But a chicken-fried night on the town might also mean drinking and shooting off bottle rockets, or drinking and knocking over mailboxes, or drinking and throwing toilet paper into a teacher's yard with a Good Old Boy looking sharp in jeans and an FFA jacket. Whether he's a Gentleman or a Good Old Boy, urbane or charmingly small town, the young Southern man's social-romantic agenda hinges on getting mentally muddied enough to have sex. Down here, wherever belles get drunk, beaus congregate waiting eagerly for one to fall.

They don't usually have to wait for long, because Southern belles have managed to gain a reputation as the most pure and, at the same time, most prurient women on the planet. How? Writer Florence King—a wise old belle her ownself—observed that Southern girls simply erase

1841 The Citadel military academy is established at Charleston, South Carolina.

9

sex acts. Here's how: If it's not premeditated, it didn't happen. If the deflowering took place in the car, in the darkness, or in the woods, it didn't happen. If you weren't both completely naked, it wasn't making love, and so you will still, in a sense, be a virgin on your wedding night. And, well, if you were drunk, it might have happened, but it didn't really count. Using this ingenious little device, a Southern girl can come home with her panties in her pocketbook *and* her virtue intact.

While the belle fudges the facts about her chastity, the beau

HOT SOUTHERN TEEN SEX

A FELLOW picks up his date. They go get a hamburger at the drive-in and talk for a while. He'll have a bottle of Jack Daniel's stashed under the seat of his pickup to spruce up the Cokes. By the time the carhop comes to fetch the tray, both young lovebirds are snockered. Soon they're smooching by the light of the moon.

With the spooning comes some seriously euphemistic love talk. He asks: "You want to go somewhere?" He means: "You want to go park in the woods and wiggle out of that brassiere?"

He interprets the shrug of her shoulders as "yes." So, they head to the cemetery, the Goat Man Road, or the abandoned hotel at the edge of town where several other cars hover in the darkness with windshields already fogged. He kills the lights, and they pretend to debate. "I don't know," she wavers. "It's late, and I think I might be getting cramps or –"

He cuts her off. "I just wanted to hold you for a little bit. I just want to be close, and just, you know, just talk. That's all." They chug a little more Jack, this time without any Coke. She turns up the radio. They kiss some more. He manages to open her blouse. Soon it's off completely. After quite a bit of fumbling, he unhooks her bra.

She stops. "It's late. Maybe we should go," she teases.

"I have a blanket and some pillows in the truck bed," he says as if he just so happens to carry a bedroll with him at all times. "Let's just get back there and just look at the stars."

They climb into the truck's cargo area and don't waste a minute gazing skyward. After a few more heavy breaths, she squirms out of her T-shirt. "You got something?" she asks. Something in this situation being Southern-talk for condom. He doesn't. She rolls her eyes and calls him a dweeb. She takes another hit of bourbon and goes for his zipper. He stops her.

"Oh, damn!" he thinks. "I thought she was a nice girl."

A BRIEF HISTORY OF SOUTHERN MANHOOD, continues

employs some artful exaggeration in the other direction. Virginal Southern women carry value, virginal Southern men carry stigmas. The Southern girl must somehow retain a vestige of virtue even after marriage, but the Southern boy must shake all remnants of his as soon as possible. Keeping in mind that it takes two to tango, but one isn't allowed to dance and the other isn't allowed to admit inexperience, is it any wonder Southern courtship makes for such comic choreography? Sex, Florence King wrote, is the only American invention that doesn't save time and trouble.

Once you get past the frustrating complexities of the mating dance, falling in love or lust with a Southern man has a definite bright side. The Southern woman holds a reputation for being devious in matters of romance, but she never has to hoodwink a Dixie fellow to get him horizontal. Just try making a cobra stay away from a flute.

My mother once told me that Southern men don't care about kissing or hugging; they just want somebody to take care of them. I think Mama was wrong. In love, the Southern boy can be both swashbuckling and sensitive. He likes to talk and he *loves* to kiss. Oh, he'll sprinkle Yankee dimes over lips, ears, hands, even feet for hours in an attempt to unfreeze an icy belle. Think about it. Nobody but a Southern boy like Conway Twitty could have recorded "Slow Hand" and not been accused of distributing pornography.

In his fantasy, the Southern man fully understands women. In real life, he remains perpetually confused. I met a Good Old Boy in a French Quarter bar who offered a parable to explain this confusion. "When I was a boy," he said, "this big kid in the neighborhood bloodied my nose. I went running home to Mama. She got mad—*mad at me!* 'No matter who it is, and no matter how big, you stand up for yourself when somebody does you wrong,' she said. 'You fight like a man next time.' Very

BUMPER STICKER

DON'T COME A KNOCKIN' IF THE VAN'S A ROCKIN'!

FINDING MISS ALMOST RIGHT

*T**HE AVERAGE** Southern man could overlook a harelip on the woman who makes him feel special and loved.*

One guy—divorced, middle aged, and recently returned to the dating circuit—proved the point. Believing himself to be quite the playboy, he talked a good story about the glamorous women making his social calendar sizzle, until he finally fell in love. In describing his new honey to his adult daughter, the gentleman said: "Sweet, smart, and pretty too. Just my type." He hesitated for a moment, then added, "And I know she's not an albino, because I asked her."

A BRIEF HISTORY OF SOUTHERN MANHOOD, continues

BIG TIMES IN SMALL TOWNS

- Following the volunteer fire department to a fire.
- Sitting on the hood of the car outside a Holy Roller tent revival.
- Necking.
- Watching the bug zapper work its magic.
- Waving at passenger trains.

next day, a big old girl in the neighborhood started picking on me. So I hauled off and hit her. Mama came running out of the house and whupped the tar out of me. 'Mama! Mama!' I screamed. 'I'm standing up for myself, just like you said.' Mama glared at me, and said, 'Don't you ever, never let me catch you hitting a girl again, you hear?' "

The fellow swallowed some more whiskey and grinned like a mule eating briars. "And y'all wonder why Southern men grow up confused by women?"

Many a Southern marriage functions an awful lot like the relationship between Darin and Samantha Stevens on *Bewitched.* Remember? He was a geeky mortal, and she a seductive good witch. Just like Darin, the Southern man marries a woman more powerful than he is, yet as if by magic she remains content to live in his shadow. It's true. The sexes flip psychologically cattywampus in Dixie.

Inside the dainty bosom of the Southern woman beats the heart of a fearless lion, and cowering behind the Southern man's facade of invincibility flutters a sensitive lamb likely to lapse into hysteria any time his ego sustains a scratch. When a Southern man's self-image comes under fire, fetch the smelling salts. It's Ashley, not Scarlett, who's prone to swoon.

Since belles are susceptible to egomania, and Southern Gentlemen struggle with insecurity, as a couple their neuroses cancel each other out. When he's running low on confidence, she fills his tank with a bit of her overflow. Together they form an almost balanced personality.

"A good wife is a first step toward greatness," Southern daddies tell their boys. For some boys that first step is the only one he has to worry his pretty little head about, 'cause the Mrs. will take it from there. The groom's role at the wedding ceremony rates as a cameo at best. And whether he takes his bride to Europe on the Concorde or leaves the driving to Greyhound when he and his beloved head for Dollywood, the Southern man usually gets his first taste of eternity before he's had a chance to digest the wedding cake.

If only the Dixie boy could get his beer to cool as fast as his sex life does once the honeymoon's over. He takes up golf. She joins the Junior League. But true to his word, the kingly Southern man treats his spouse in the odd way *he deems* befitting a queen.

Before his marriage, a longtime Charleston bachelor kept his clothes neatly sorted in two hampers, one for the dirties and one for the cleans. When the clean hamper emptied, he knew it was time to wash. On the Monday morning after his wedding trip, this guy noticed that both hampers were empty. He found all his underwear neatly folded in a drawer, his socks in another. He said to his new wife: "Do you mean you'll be doing this every day? I should have gotten married a long time ago!"

As a newlywed, he became accustomed to his wife sectioning his grapefruit every morning. One day, when she failed to do this for him, the wife caught him sitting at the table, hands in his lap, just staring at his breakfast. "It's not sectioned," he said seriously. "How do I eat it if it's not sectioned?"

That same man's wife heard somewhere that the happier a marriage, the sooner a widow or widower remarries following the death of a spouse. "I'm telling y'all, we're so happy he'll be slipping into his tuxedo if I even take sick."

Sure, plenty of Southern marriages stand as solid as Rock City. But even in beautiful Beulahland sometimes things go wrong before death parts a pair of lovebirds. These days unions fail almost as often as NASA space missions, and the only spectacle grander and more imaginative than the Southern wedding is the Southern divorce. When sweet romance suddenly goes sour, the Southern couple hits the abort-marriage button, and the fur starts to fly.

"I'm fixing to file on your ass!" is the war cry of the unhappy Southern bride. The actual filing of motions at the courthouse doesn't make for juicy *Divorce Court* drama nearly so much as the stuff that precedes the first call to the lawyer. Dixie-bred humorist Bo Whaley once wrote that he was all for women's liberation. He'd liberated one himself in court.

A BRIEF HISTORY OF SOUTHERN MANHOOD, continues

Breakups can be confusing for the Southern man. He picks up an outright violent message with crystal clarity, no problem. But he's perpetually baffled by the passive assault of the wronged Southern belle. A belle will never, ever slap a man. Instead, she makes him punch drunk with praise and then takes his most beloved bird dog to the pound. Or she serves his favorite dinner, then goes outside and smashes his antique Thunderbird to dust with a sledgehammer while he's eating. Or she makes mad passionate love to him, then steps into the bathroom to freshen up and is never seen or heard from again.

When a former coworker of mine suspected that her steady boyfriend was two-timing her, she went out and bought a big piece of calf's liver and an ice pick. Then she scrawled CALL ME, YOU ASSHOLE on a piece of paper and used the ice pick to pin the liver and the note to her sweetheart's front door. He called. Three days later he proposed. Today they couldn't be happier.

Occasionally a girl needs a two-by-four to get a man's attention, but in the long run with a Southern man, it's usually worth the trouble. He might not talk about his feelings or remember to pick up his dirty underwear off the bathroom floor, but the Southerner usually behaves like a gentleman and he never loses interest in romance.

In the small Southern town where I grew up, two men who had enjoyed a lifelong friendship and served together in World War I neared the end of their road. I mean these guys were old—in their late eighties or early nineties. One gentleman lay near death in a hospital bed, and his frail friend kept a bedside vigil. After several days lapsing in and out of a coma, the dying man suddenly regained consciousness. Reaching through the tangle of tubes and cords connecting him to life, the patient grasped his buddy's hand and managed the words, "Bobby? That you?"

"Yeah, Ed," Bobby responded, wiping a tear from his eye. "It's me."

"Hey, Bobby," Ed wheezed. "Remember that stuff they gave us during the war to make us not interested in women?"

"Yeah, I remember," Bobby answered. "Seems like they called it saltpeter."

"Well"—Ed managed a faint smile—"I think it's finally starting to kick in."

CHAPTER TWO

Hellfire
&
Damnation

Jesus Wants Him for a Sunbeam

B OYS AND GIRLS, DO ANY OF Y'ALL HAVE A FAVORITE Bible verse you'd like to share?"
A friend remembers a Mr. Rogers-like Sunday School teacher asking this one morning as she and her friends cut out construction-paper animals to go in a cardboard replica of Noah's ark.

One goody two-shoes said his favorite verse was "The Lord is my shepherd. I shall not want."

"Jesus wept," cited another future pastor.

Finally one boy raised his hand and blurted out Proverbs 26:11, his Biblical numero uno: A fool returns to his folly, like a dog returns to his *vomit.*

The class howled with laughter. The teacher issued the rascal a spanking.

To most Southerners, religion isn't funny. When John Lennon made a desultory remark about the decline of religion and the Beatles rivaling the popularity of Jesus, Southerners weren't laughing. In Birmingham, Alabama, they set up drop-off points for Beatles paraphernalia. Not many Bible Belters ever found the humor in the HONK IF YOU ARE JESUS parodies of the original HONK IF YOU LOVE JESUS bumper stickers either. When the American Atheist Press published an X-rated version of the Bible to "expose obscenity in Christendom's most holy work," Southerners were disgusted. The typical Southland family says grace before a meal even when they're breaking bread at Bonanza. The point? Dixie boys take religion very, very seriously. They have strong and faith-filled hearts. And that's good news for belles most of the time.

Student lore at one Southern military school tells of a boy who sneaked a girl up to his dorm room one night for a little hanky-panky. A group of underclassmen saw the pair duck upstairs and decided to serenade them. Standing below the open window the choristers sang "Jesus Loves Me" and other mood-killing hymns. The boy upstairs couldn't take it. He repented, zipped up, and ratted on himself.

Like the preacher says, "There are always signs for those with eyes to see." Homemade GET RIGHT WITH GOD placards dot rural Southern highways. Along a winding farm road near my hometown, I once passed a series of crudely lettered roadside posters. Like the old Burma Shave signs, each contained one word: DON'T. YOU. WISH. YOU. HAD. OF. TOOK. YOUR. FAMILY. TO. CHURCH? Bad grammar, but good intentions. Even in big cities it's not unusual to see a billboard advertising salvation. A giant finger points skyward and the slogan beckons ONE WAY TO HEAVEN.

THE FRONT PORCH:
Evil

NOT LONG AGO pollsters discovered that 72 percent of all Southerners believe Satan exists. You can bet if the Devil lives, he's probably up to mischief, and that means E–V–I–L.

Foreigners selling lewd postcards—that's Evil. Spitting on the graves of our heroic veterans—that's Evil. Disrespecting your mama, mistreating animals, stealing Gideon Bibles out of motel rooms, men wearing earrings—Evil, Evil, Evil, and Evil.

Old Scratch, Beelzebub, Nick. Southerners have as many names for the Devil as that Devil has tricks up his sleeves. Right-living Dixie boys realize that Satan can be one crafty adversary. The good guys have got to keep a constant vigil.

Luckily, members of one Southern school board were on the case not long ago, when the Prince of Darkness tried to spoil Christmas. Acting fast, board members foiled his Grinch-like plan. They directed that all Santa's pictures be removed from classrooms because the letters in the word SANTA can be rearranged to spell—yep, you guessed it—SATAN. But then again, DEVIL spelled backward is LIVED, and ELVIS spelled sideways is EVILS. It just goes to show that the Lord is not the only one working in mysterious ways.

A BRIEF HISTORY OF SOUTHERN MANHOOD, continues

The route to Heaven doesn't concern the Southern man nearly as much as the fare. The Good Old Boy's love of leisure gives him plenty of time to ponder eternity and the ticket prices at the Pearly Gates. Sometimes those pesky Questions Without Answers lodge themselves in the Southern Gentleman's mind too. As a result, the good-time Dixie boy's thoughts never wander far from the piper and his fee. Down South, salvation and life after death are cut-and-dried. On these matters, there is no leeway. You're either Saved or Damned, period. Jesus doesn't redshirt; a fellow's either on the Lord's team, or he's not.

Part of the subtle beauty of Southern manhood lies in how he manages to have such a grand, debauched old time and still cling to stringent notions of morality. Think about the signs. Those portable ones with the movable letters on them that you see parked in front of convenience stores. The message on one side might bark JESUS SAVES, while the other could well whisper COLD CASE O' BEER $8.

Hedonism and piety run daily schedules on parallel tracks in Dixie. When an out-of-town evangelist held a revival for teens at the high-school football stadium in my hometown, he offered free pizza and Coca-Cola to each kid who dedicated his or her life to Christ. The converts then spiked the Cokes with bourbon and started necking under the grandstands.

"Pious partyer" is not an oxymoron below the Mason-Dixon. The Southern man is sincerely both. He enjoys getting powerful drunk and then getting powerful saved. Each feels so much better when chased by the other. In other words, the rowdier a guy's Saturday night, the more humble his Sunday morning. He wallows with the hogs, and then, with eyes like Georgia road maps, he soars with the eagles. He stands for all that is good, and he apologizes weekly for not having achieved it personally. Somewhere in his heart lurks the sense that a good word cancels out an evil deed. Sinning, confessing, and sinning again. That's the way a Southerner kills time while he waits around for Armageddon.

A study conducted in the 1970s found that 72 percent of Southerners felt pretty sure that Satan existed, as compared with only 29 percent of non-Southerners.

101 USES FOR KUDZU

77—Halloween costume.

In fact, more Southerners polled believed in Satan than believed in God. So sure of Satan was one Southern man that he chugalugged twelve glasses of water real fast trying to flush the devil from his system. He died of water intoxication.

What right-thinking Good Old Boy would want to spend eternity in the Unhappy Hunting Ground, a place ten times hotter than Louisiana in July, where a guy more annoying than a Yankee know-it-all pokes at him with a pitchfork until the end of time? It doesn't take graduate work to figure out that Heaven sounds like your better deal.

Heaven is a Southern place: clouds like bolls of cotton and a gentleman holding the door. "They've got flowers there you've never seen before," my grandpa once told me. "Everything is green—without any fertilizer, just green and blooming year around. And the streets, I've heard, are paved with diamonds and gold."

Straightforward attitudes about Good and Evil pique the Dixie boys interested in the Big Picture and then gruesome visions of the apocalypse close the sale. Southern preachers tell macabre stories about the fate awaiting those outside the circle of salvation come Judgment Day.

When Ted Turner launched CNN, he reportedly mapped out the network's coverage of the End of the World. Rumor has it that during the ultimate news bulletin, a tape of military bands playing "Nearer My God to Thee" will air automatically just in case any unsaved heathen survives to watch. Nobody dares doubt the sincerity of Turner's beliefs; the programming obviously isn't intended as a ratings ploy.

In observing some elaborate freeway construction, a gentleman of my acquaintance shook his head and said: "They'll never finish these roads. The end time's coming. But if you think about it too much, you'll

GET THEE TO BATON ROUGE

G OD SPEAKS directly to Southerners. The Lord warned a preacher in Texas that the Devil was after him and his family, but God advised him not to panic. The voice from Heaven instructed the preacher and his kin to give the Devil the slip by getting naked and driving to Louisiana. The fellow put his trust in the Lord and his clothes in the trunk. Police apprehended a speeding 1990 Pontiac near Vinton filled with fifteen naked adults and five nude children.

A BRIEF HISTORY OF SOUTHERN MANHOOD, continues

1864   Sherman burns Atlanta.   Confederates try to burn New York City.

go crazy just like my Uncle Brother did. Best thing is to lead a clean life, go to church, and follow the rules."

And the Southern man does just that. He strives to keep the Ten Commandments, to follow the Golden Rule, and to make it to church on Sunday. But what sort of church? The religious Southerner will point out that there's more than one way to get square with God. The Southern Gentleman prefers a subdued service with some Latin words thrown into the liturgy and a few old-world Anglican hymns. When the Good Old Boy suits up on Sunday, he favors redemption served up in a down-home, fundamentalist setting complete with philandering polyester-clad preacher, grape-juice communion, and Holy Rollers speaking in tongues.

The Good Old Boy never has to be dragged kicking and screaming to church. He kicks and screams *at* church. He enjoys the spectacle. He rates the music as danceable as anything on *American Bandstand.* The girls look pretty, and more likely than not the sermon hits home. Besides, the football game doesn't come on till noon anyway.

Fundamentalism can be fun once you get the hang of it. A few basics: Baptism outranks communion on the stairway to heaven; the preacher puts more emphasis on saving souls than worshipping God; the sermon carries an electrical charge; the preacher refers to Jesus as if he lives right down the road. And if a fundamentalist minister delivers a talk that doesn't elicit lively participation from his congregation, he's in the wrong business. A congregation that fails to respond to good fire-and-brimstone is either already in the hands of Satan or comatose.

You'll find the really red-hot religious rhetoric unfolding in an "auditorium" rather than a "sanctuary." And for good reason. Some Southern Baptist church membership rolls exceed the population of small towns. In Memphis, Bellevue Baptist lists more than 22,000 members. And in Houston, Second Baptist, "the mega church," offers much more than plain old-fashioned spiritual nourishment. Members can attend Sunday School,

H E R O E S O F T H E C L O T H

Billy Graham
Martin Luther King, Jr.
Grady Nutt
Jimmy Swaggart
George Foreman
Oral Roberts
Jerry Falwell
Pat Robertson
Jim Bakker
Jesse Jackson

work out at the health club, see a movie in the theater, and bowl a few frames without leaving the Lord's House.

Instead of hosting bingo, these congregations pass the collection plate by way of spaghetti suppers. Church elders vote to spend the tithe on sound systems or electric guitars instead of Last Supper mosaics or marble Pietàs. Unlike cathedrals or synagogues, the Good Old Boy's house of worship has no great works of religious art. There's no need for it. In Protestant fundamentalism, the spirit zooms right past the believer's eyes and finds the way to his soul through his ears.

Brothers and sisters, good music and lively preaching carry the message. Hallelujah! That's what makes Holy Roller services just perfect for TV. It takes a big personality, bright colors, and plenty of hairspray to bring the Word into millions of homes via satellite. The key component of Jimmy Swaggart chic is an Easter egg–blue suit made from a fabric that would melt should the reverend ever backslide and light a cigarette. It's an off-the-rack vestment more the color of a coconut snow cone than the uniform of the British navy. When he accessorizes with white vinyl shoes, white belt, Porter Wagoner hairdo, clip-on tie, and short-sleeved shirt—praise the Lord!—he's practically flashing the prayer-line number on the screen already.

Electronic churches are like tent revivals gone high tech. Oral Roberts, Pat Robertson, Jerry Falwell. Heavens! There are more Southern preachers on TV than talk-show hosts. And they're not just reading from the Good Book twenty-four hours a day either. He who toucheth the imagination along with the conscience and the pocketbook thrives. When not in the pulpit, Pat Robertson hosts a news program, and CBN broadcasts a Christian soap opera. Although you've got to wonder how they maintain viewership with no adultery in the plot line.

TICKETS TO HEAVEN

In a fund-raising effort, one small-town Methodist minister mailed each member of his congregation a mock concert ticket. Each ticket read:

SEAT: Right hand of God
ROW: Straight and narrow
GATES: Pearly

1865 The unthinkable: a sad, sad day at Appomattox in April.

Follow. Yield. Surrender. Those verbs figure heavily in the televangelist's liturgy. Southern Baptists and Pentecostals and other fundamentalist denominations share a belief that faith operates on an emotional rather than an intellectual plane. The Good Old Boy isn't educated into Christendom. It strikes him like a bolt from heaven in a personal way.

No matter how open his heart, the fundamentalist's mind likely stays closed. He's not comfortable with newfangled ideas. Evolution, for example, really riles the Dixie faithful. Remember the Scopes monkey trials from *Inherit the Wind*? In the movie *Elmer Gantry*, a smooth-talking evangelist plays with a cute chimp and tells the congregation: "This might be Darwin's uncle, but not mine, brothers and sisters, not mine."

School prayer gets under his skin too. Even though the Supreme Court ruled praying in schools to be unconstitutional, Southerners do it anyway because they know God is on their side. "Bootleg prayer," they call it. "When prayers are outlawed, only outlaws will say prayers."

VOODOO

VOODOO IS PART folk religion and part folk medicine, although its medicinal aspects are not always used to heal.

For example, in Tupelo two brothers went to trial for trying to kill a judge using a voodoo hex. The boys had hired a mojo hit man from Jamaica to issue the whammy. The judge's wife got suspicious when the brothers called to ask for a photo of the judge and some of his hair.

Voodoo "doctors" use spells and herbal remedies in their practice. They work up a mojo—a small sack containing dead insects, lizards, and parts of clothes or hair from the person being cursed—as a vehicle for the spell. "High John the Conqueror root" is the nuclear weapon in the voodoo doctor's arsenal. Those who understand voodoo tremble at the sight of the root's presence in the hands of others.

Voodoo practitioners never write down their methods, because the powerful knowledge could fall into the wrong hands. The craft is passed orally from generation to generation. Blues singers refer to voodoo often, and contrary to popular belief, blacks are not its only practitioners. The University of Mississippi School of Medicine has worked with voodoo doctor's to heal patients:

"Wear this mojo around your neck. Eat two hen's feet, and call me in the morning."

A BRIEF HISTORY OF SOUTHERN MANHOOD, continues

In North Carolina one such little outlaw got himself expelled for preaching at school. When the principal asked the young reverend to stop using the playground as a pulpit, the fiery ten-year-old shouted: "Woe unto you, scribes and Pharisees." Then the spirit moved his five-year-old brother, who chimed in, "Marriage is honorable in all, and the bed undefiled. But whoremongers and adulterers God will judge!"

A little bit of scripture goes a long way. Southerners realize that the Word can be powerful, like a gun, and that a child should know how to use it properly before he starts waving it around. Grown men sometimes get drunk on the power of preaching and show female members of the congregation alternate routes to Heaven. As result of a few fellows' well-publicized transgressions, all Southern clerics have suffered lately from some bad PR. As one cynical Good Old Boy explained, "Many a man has been toiling in the hot sun when the Lord called him to preach in the shade."

John Shelton Reed writes funny stuff about the region all the time. He once ran across a preaching boogie-woogie man billing himself as the "High Prophet of Polyester," the director of "Our First Lady of the White Go-Go Boots Worldwide Love Ministries, Inc." Churches don't pay taxes, you know. Clerics like the High Prophet of Polyester sometimes make it difficult for serious preachers to do their jobs.

Long before the fall of Jim and Tammy Faye, before the dalliances of Jimmy Swaggart were made public, and before Oral Roberts announced that God was going to call him home unless his viewers coughed up a few million dollars, two Southern prophets saw the whole thing coming. Chet Atkins wrote and Ray Stevens sang "Would Jesus Wear a Rolex?" on his television show.

Southerners take religion mighty seriously. They just don't lose

BUMPER STICKER

MY BEST FRIEND WAS A CARPENTER

sleep over sin. The Good Old Boy considers the man without sin a sissy. And to the Southern Gentleman, sin seems mild compared to a social faux pas. While the Good Old Boy rocks along with the toe-tapping hymns at the tent revival, the Southern Gentleman likely prays Episcopalian- or Presbyterian-style, sipping sherry with the blue-hairs after the service. Think. Consider. Understand. Those are the verbs the Episcopalian minister slings around in proving that progressive views and traditional values need not necessarily be contradictory. As the saying goes: "Episcopalianism lets you believe in anything you want, even sin." That sounds like a good deal to most Southern Gentlemen.

Where the Good Old Boy cleric wears polyester and models himself after Elmer Gantry, a Southern Gentleman of the cloth gets all excited about gold-embossed Anglican vestments and envisions himself as a character from *Chariots of Fire*. In the Gentleman's sanctuary, the communion wine carries a good vintage and is dispensed from a silver chalice. At the Good Old Boy's auditorium, the sacrament is made by Welch's and served in plastic medicine cups.

The Good Old Boy preacher allows his congregation to use trendy, easy-to-read translations of the Bible, but the Gentlemanly minister demands the King James all the way—the more *thous* and *thees* the better. The Good Old Boy preacher studied for his ordination at Bob Jones University or got his credentials through the mail from a Bible college. The Gentleman cleric memorized his liturgy at Sewanee or, better yet, at Oxford. He laces his sermons with references to Plato and quotes from John Donne. One of many reasons he loves his work is because it's almost like getting paid to be a full-time philosopher, a Cambridge don in Knoxville, Tennessee.

Baptists and Episcopalians don't hold a monopoly on Southern Sabbaths. Devotees of Catholicism and Judaism flip on the football game after worship too. (And Moravians and Quakers and just about any oth-

---

THE RIGHT ADDRESS

"God of Israel, God of the centuries, God of our forefathers, God of Jefferson Davis and Sidney Johnston and Robert E. Lee, and Stonewall Jackson, God of the Southern Confederacy."
—from a prayer used at Southern veterans' gatherings

A BRIEF HISTORY OF SOUTHERN MANHOOD, continues

er religious group you can think of, and some you can't.) Voodoo has disciples in Dixie. So does snake-handling, a religion where followers literally interpret Mark 16:18—"They shall take up serpents and if they drink any deadly thing, it shall not hurt them." Two or three nights a week the faithful gather a passel of copperheads and water moccasins and toss them into the congregation. A bite indicates a lapse in the victim's faith, but happens surprisingly infrequently.

No matter what the church affiliation, there are always signs. During a traffic jam in Tennessee several thousand motorists reported seeing the face of Jesus hanging in the air above the freeway. The face of Christ showed up on a flour tortilla in South Texas. Another such vision—"the porch light Jesus"—materialized on the side of a deep freeze on the deck of a couple's mobile home whenever their neighbor turned on his porch light. From another little town came reports of the Virgin's image on a Camaro's hood. Some others saw her silhouette on the side of a barn. But the face of Christ that came into focus on another barn in Texas turned out to be a false alarm. Instead of a miracle, it was just a faded advertisement for Willie Nelson's Fourth of July picnic.

There are always signs for those with eyes to see. Recently a few of those with eyes have been seeing Elvis, alive and well and apparently traveling quite a bit. According to the tabloids—the holy books of Elvisism—a woman claims to have spied the King buying fresh produce or something at a Michigan supermarket. Someone else spotted him on the beach in Maine. Yet another believer caught him sipping Chardonnay in the California wine country.

As always, there are skeptics, nonbelievers who get their kicks going around debunking miracles. "Lettuce and spinach? Elvis? Don't make me laugh. Maine? Too cold! Too many damn Yankees! And Chardonnay? Maybe, just maybe, with a Jack chaser."

Mostly "Elvis Lives" works as a punch line, and Southerners usually laugh along. The King of Rock 'n' Roll might merit a tongue-in-cheek velvet shrine in many a Christian household, but when Ann Landers wrote a column supporting the official line that Elvis

THE SIN SECTION

Overheard at a ticket counter in the Atlanta airport:

COUNTER CLERK: "Smoking or nonsmoking, sir?"

PASSENGER: "Smoking, drinking, talking dirty! Hell, just put us in the back with the TV preachers!"

had gone on to his final rest at Graceland, those convinced otherwise flooded her with irate mail. Since the King's last finale, his name and image have become even more pervasive in Dixie culture than during his life. These just might be the dawning years of the A.E. (After Elvis) Era. Christianity split, you'll remember. And a schism has already begun to develop in the Elvis cult.

These days one school of Elvisism hinges upon the belief "He Lives." Another faction adheres to the idea that Elvis died, but he died for our sins. The latter group disseminates the story about the Elvis paint-ing in Germany that reportedly cries real tears for the dreadful state of mankind, or maybe for the abysmal state of pop music—a rock 'n' roll stigmata, you might say. Then there's the Elvis Revelation. A psychic predicts that there'll be an earthquake in the Memphis area, hundreds will die, the tomb at Graceland will open, and its contents will be revealed. A fundamentalist Elvis disciple told a tabloid, "Elvis is up in Heaven right now talking to me and other people like me who care so deeply about him. When I have a problem, I ask God for guidance and He hands me over to Elvis, who is one of God's right-hand men. Like all angels, he inspires people." Amen.

CHAPTER THREE

The Way to a Man's Heart

Corn, Hog, and All Things Fried or Distilled

Y ANKEE CULINARY SNOBS GET THEIR KICKS BY saying that a seven-course meal in the South is a six-pack and a dead possum.

Well, most any Southerner will point out that a Yankee knows about as much about good eating as a hog knows about the Lord's plan for salvation. The difference is, the hog doesn't *think* he knows.

Despite what the occasional EAT MORE POSSUM bumper sticker suggests, only the most cash-strapped Southerners chow down on marsupials these days. And when pressed, or threatened with bodily harm, Yankees and most other Americans will reluctantly admit that the cuisine Southern boys were weaned on represents the culinary soul of the nation.

Whether he sits down at the mahogany dining-room table of an antebellum plantation or scoots up to the glass-and-chrome dinette in a brand-new mobile home, the Southern man is keen on good grub. He gobbles up biscuits, watermelon, fried chicken. He'll spend hours debating the best combination of fuel and basting to produce a perfectly barbecued hog. When Southern men aren't talking about cars or women, they're likely swapping barbecue stories or tackling important gastronomic issues such as "Mayonnaise vs. Miracle Whip: Which goes best on a potato chip sandwich?"

Of course, it's not like the average Southern guy won't eat pretty much anything put in front of him. He actually likes the butter flavoring on picture-show popcorn, and he thinks that always-melted nacho cheese served at the ballpark is just the greatest thing since sliced bread. In fact, he wonders how it would taste *with* sliced bread.

Dixie boys believe that life is for living, that there will be plenty of time to diet and feel guilty in the grave. Your West Coast ponytails might belly up to a water bar and order up a bottle of designer burps, but down here if a guy's going to the trouble to belly up, he wants a drink that'll warm his innards and have him crawling home. Yogurt and granola might make a power breakfast for the tassel-loafer types in Manhattan, but a power breakfast for the Sansabelt set down in Macon involves fat and cholesterol—with gravy.

Grown men networking at Alcoholics Anonymous meetings? Not in Dixie. Why would anybody pay good money to vacation in Arizona at a health spa where you can't eat anything but lettuce or drink anything but carrot juice? Well, it's just beyond the Southern man's understand-

THE FRONT PORCH:
Pork

*T*O THE SOUTHERN GENTLEMAN's *way of thinking, if there's not pork on the table, a meal has been emasculated. He'll have bacon for breakfast, barbecued ribs for his noontime dinner, and then cuddle up to a ham sandwich and molasses on light bread for his supper. And don't even get him going about barbecue. The barbecue-recipe gene comes on the Y chromosome. Every man breathing below the Mason–Dixon has his own scientific method for cooking meat. "I'll bet I could make Jimmy Hoffa taste good with a light brushing of my secret sauce."*

Westerners may swear by barbecued beef, but Southerners get high on the hog. In the parlance of the Old South, "high on the hog" meant something similar to "living large" because the affluent planter's family typically dined on a porker's choicer top cuts, with the less desirable pig parts feeding the staff. Ham might make a better meal than pig's feet, but when a hog squeals its last in Dixie nothing goes to waste. Its fat becomes lard. Its bladder, though inedible, can be filled with air to make a great balloon-like toy for the kids to kick around in the yard. And the pig's skin? Football. The Southern man's favorite dinner and his number-one game spring from the same porcine source.

A BRIEF HISTORY OF SOUTHERN MANHOOD, continues

ing, that's all. As one Good Old Boy says, "Eating rabbit food is no kind of life for a man." He appreciates earthly pleasures and sees no reason to deny himself. The Southerner never forgets that the first end in life is living itself.

In the newspaper not long ago, I saw an article about a man in Argentina who ate an entire hog at a single sitting. When he finished, he took a nap and never woke up again. I told a friend about this, and he said, "Wow! What a fine way to go!"

In the South, gluttony is good. The Southerner respects excess and plenty of it. Remember Jolt Cola— "All the sugar, twice the caffeine"? I'd bet more than just Confederate money that Jolt sold well in the South. John Shelton Reed thinks that if the tobacco industry ever got serious about selling smokes to Good Old Boys "they'd bring out something like 'Death' cigarettes—all the nicotine, twice the tar." To the large-living Southerners' way of thinking, fatty food, potent drink, and the high-quality visitation that usually accompanies both make for a rich, full life.

It's not unusual around these parts to hear about a hungry man harpooning his own child's hand in a race for the last pork chop on the platter. The Good Old Boy loves to pack in the calories, and while the sybaritic Southern Gentleman might lack the Good Old Boy's trophy gut, he's no stranger to overindulgence his ownself. No, ma'am. His form of indulgence is liquid, and he's got the ruddy complexion to prove it. He wears his badge of hedonism in the broken blood vessels on his face.

The way to a Southern fellow's heart is most definitely through his stomach. Corn, pork, and all things fried or distilled blaze the way. Whether he's a belching Good Old Boy or a hiccuping Southern Gentleman, he lives hand-to-mouth, and the hand is usually a blur. No matter how educated, how well traveled, or how refined his palate, any Southern man handed a bag of shelled peanuts and a Dr Pepper will automatically drop the nuts into the soda, shake it up, and chugalug. Pickled pigs feet in a jar of pink vinegar? He'll take two, to go. The Southern gourmet might sip Puligny-Montrachet or order the duck with mango-pine nut chutney at a fancy Atlanta restaurant, but buy him a Slim Jim meat

101 USES FOR KUDZU
#51—Salad greens.

A BRIEF HISTORY OF SOUTHERN MANHOOD, continues

stick and he'll know what to do. Suck the grease out of the end and savor every mmm-good bite.

From Jimmy Carter to Grandpa Jones, all Southern males claim some degree of expertise in matters gastronomic. Even so, there's scarcely a man-child breathing in Dixie who has not at some time or the other considered a chili-cheese dog from the Stop 'n' Go to be brunch. He's goofy for Goo Goo Clusters, pie-eyed for Moon Pies, and believes Yoo-Hoo makes a dandy breakfast drink. "It's like café au lait, except cheaper."

Even in this day of low-fat mania, "fry" remains the rebellious Southern man's favorite—no, make that *second* favorite—verb. He won't eat what he can't pronounce, and he shuns some things he can say just fine, such as "cucumber sandwich." He stays away from Yankeeland standards such as spanakopita, vichyssoise, and rata-touille. He avoids low-fat dishes like a heart attack, and refuses most any item served cold. Put a bowl of gazpacho in front of him, and he'll make a face, asking "Did the cat fall into the blender?"

The Jack Spratt Diet won't float around here. As the Southern man sees it, the words "heart smart" translate as "no fun." He believes that bacon grease keeps the joints from squeaking. He cozies up to a big old cholesterol feed like a snake slithers for kudzu. Even when his arterial blockage approaches danger levels, he'll crow for eggs any style, especially deviled. He'd rather choke on feathers than try one of those weird egg substitutes. But your typical Southern man does make a stab at what he considers to be a balanced diet. At mealtime

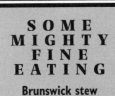

SOME MIGHTY FINE EATING

Brunswick stew
Burgoo
Pot likker
Chitlins
Catfish
Hushpuppies
Grits
Biscuits
Poke salad
Okra
Collards
Sweet potatoes
Barbecue
Boudin
Red beans and rice
Crawdads
Fried chicken
Squirrel and dumplings
Stone crab
Grits
Country ham
Moon Pie

he's careful to include selections from his version of the four basic food groups: alcohol, grease, sugar, and salt.

When grazing the Basic Four, the Southerner can't help playing favorites. Those favorites form the staples of Southern cuisine. List corn on the Dixie Deal-a-Meal Diet Plan as a serving from the salt group, and pork comes under grease. To this day, corn and pork combine to make up the greater part of most Southerners' daily menus.

Somebody told me once that the language of the Eskimos contains about thirty different words for snow. So when you think about it, it's not all that surprising that the parlance of the American Southerner boasts at least twelve different ways to say corn and almost that many for pig.

Senator Strom Thurmond once said that Southerners enjoy corn in most any form, includ-ing "by the glass." It's true. From corn liquor to corn bread to corn pone to corn on the cob, Southerners sure love to shuck. They call ultimate corn, self-actualized corn, corn at the top of the evolutionary ladder "grits." When Southern-ers sing the praises of grits, they're not dis-cussing ground-in dirt, chutzpah, or moxie. They're talking hominy, the glue that holds Southern society togeth-er.

Grits have gone uptown lately. A man can find them almost anywhere these days. Like many foods of the South, grits were once associated with poverty

A BRIEF HISTORY OF SOUTHERN MANHOOD, continues

and hard times. But today grits grace fancy hotel breakfast menus from Memphis to Milan. As one Southerner said after ordering an herbal-garlic grits soufflé at a restaurant in Manhattan: "There's something just not right about charging a man $10 for something as essential to life as grits." After spending $15 for a "Southern breakfast" up North, one Beulah boy said he expected the deed to the restaurant along with his change.

In New York City or anywhere else you might come across a Southerner far from home, just try casually bringing up grits in conversation. The Southerner's drawl will pick up an extra lilt as he describes the just-right way to serve the down-home breakfast gravel. Mention grits with ham or grits with bacon and you'll have made a friend for life.

Most Southerners cannot fathom life without pork. A young Baptist man from Arkansas quizzed a new Dixie-born Jewish friend at college about keeping kosher. "So you're telling me that y'all don't eat pork—not even ham?" the Baptist asked, incredulous.

"That's right, not even ham," replied the Jew.

The Baptist shook his head in disbelief. "If you can't have ham, what do y'all eat at Easter?"

The only imaginable hog-based dish that your average Good Old Boy could even con-template refusing would be "pork sushi," and if he was hungry enough, he might give even that a whirl. Things have a natural order, the Southerner believes, and mixing and matching certain foods amounts to tampering with the balance of nature. He likes okra, for example, but not as an ice-cream flavoring. Jalapeño jelly makes no sense to him whatsoever. "I wouldn't put it on a wart, much less in my mouth."

A fellow I know in Louisiana, already a good bit agitated by all this "nouvelle Southern cuisine crap," reached his boiling point when he spotted a road sign hawking CRAWFISH FLAN. He pulled over to set things

A   B O Y   A N D   H I S   H O G

IN THE BIG THICKET of East Texas, one Southern Gentleman's passion for pork extends beyond barbecue. From a young age he has prized pig flesh, living pig flesh.

When this man was a boy, his grandfather awarded him a piglet of his very own to fatten and tend. Each day the boy slopped the hog and monitored its growth. He named the critter "Pig Ears" for a reason unclear to all except himself, and developed quite a friendship with his porcine charge. It was the classic tale with a Southern twist—"A Boy and His Hog."

Finally the day dawned when the boy and his grandfather hauled Pig Ears to the slaughterhouse. Seemingly oblivious that his pet would soon be bacon, the boy took the $35 he got from the sale and bought himself a brand-new bicycle down at Western Auto. After several hours with the new bike, the boy said to his grandfather, "Should we go get Pig Ears now? It's almost time for his supper."

When Pig Ears' fate was explained, the boy became inconsolable. A call to the slaughterhouse came too late for a stay of execution, but the butcher had saved the animal's tail. Would that help? It would.

Every day for several weeks after Pig Ears' demise, the boy demanded that his mother pin the curly tail on the back of his blue jeans before kindergarten, and every night before bedtime he carefully placed the tail in the refrigerator for safekeeping.

Twenty years after Pig Ears headed up to the Big Sty in the Sky, this young man bought another porker. After several months, the new hog choked on a pop-tab from a soda can, leaving the man just as bereaved as he'd been before, only now he was too old to wear the tail. Today the fellow remains strangely attracted to the pig arena at livestock shows and admits, "I can't help it. I'm just queer for pigs."

DRINKING DRY

Southerners will vote dry
as long as they can stagger to the polls.
—Will Rogers

straight with whatever Yankee Communist had the gall to go advertising something so, so un-American. While fishing around in the back of his truck for a sledgehammer, the ticked-off Good Old Boy noticed on second reading that the sign said CRAWFISH FARM. He bought ten pounds.

Around here when a guy insists "I'm a meat-and-potatoes man," he means he's not interested in sampling the cuisine of a foreign country or in seeing a wad of goat cheese plopped on his mashed potatoes. Even though he'll pass on the crudité, he seldom minds seeing some salty collards or okra or black-eyed peas or snap beans on his plate as long as they've been cooked to a mush in pot likker. He might pick the bacon bits off the top of a green salad as long as it doesn't have something ridiculous like pear roquefort dressing poured all over it. There is one salad the Southern man truly loves. It's the one that combines marshmallows, canned fruit cocktail, and Cool Whip. He likes it with little powdered sugar doughnuts—instead of Melba toasts—on the side.

Even though he may sniff around a meal pretending he's a discriminating gourmand, the Southern eater is a survivalist more than anything else. When times turn tough—and in Dixie they always do—the resourceful Southerner fresh out of chewing tobacco will suck a wad of instant coffee and teach his boy to stretch Red Man by mixing it with bubble gum. Around here a man absolutely believes that "God'll get you for wasting food"; it ranks way up there on the list of cardinal sins. That's why the Southern man always cooks what he kills. When a man who lived near the town where I grew up came home drunk one night and mistook a stray dog for a bobcat, he shot it. Realizing what he'd done, he did not hesitate. He skinned the pooch, fried it, and ate it with cream gravy and biscuits, insisting "You kill it, you cook it, you eat it. It's just not right to let meat rot."

Resourceful, yes; stupid, no. Contrary to Yankee propaganda, the Southerner is no more likely to eat dirt than anyone else on the planet—

A BRIEF HISTORY OF SOUTHERN MANHOOD, continues

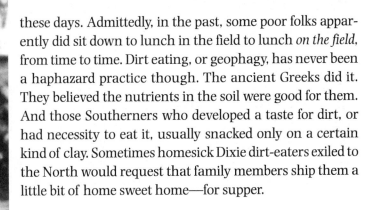

THE GLUE THAT HOLDS THE SOUTH TOGETHER

G RITS MAY BE the first truly American food. In the spring of 1607, Indians welcomed English settlers to Jamestown, Virginia, with hot, steaming bowls of what they called "rockahominie." The colonists Anglicized it to "hominy," or just plain grits. Finer than the kernels on the ear, but not as powdery as cornmeal, grits result from the milling of corn. Dried, hulled kernels treated with lye are pulverized into grits. Or regular hard corn can be coarsely ground and sifted to become grits. Southern cooks make grits with cheese, grits with garlic, grits with gravy, grits with peanut butter, grits with raisins, and even grits with caviar. Grits follow the sunrise most mornings in Dixie whether requested or not.

As a salute to the Southern breakfast of champions, filmmaker Stan Woodward produced a short documentary called It's Grits. With camera rolling, he went around asking famous and not-so-famous Southerners, "Do you eat grits?"

"Sure," most folks answered, looking at Woodward like he was some sort of lunatic. "Of course I eat grits. Don't you?"

"Grits: singular or plural?" People from other places ask Southerners this, almost always thinking it a clever query. Southerners, to tell the truth, could care less about the numerative case of grits. When asked, "Grits: singular or plural?" the Good Old Boy's response is likely to be "Grits? Where?"

these days. Admittedly, in the past, some poor folks apparently did sit down to lunch in the field to lunch *on the field*, from time to time. Dirt eating, or geophagy, has never been a haphazard practice though. The ancient Greeks did it. They believed the nutrients in the soil were good for them. And those Southerners who developed a taste for dirt, or had necessity to eat it, usually snacked only on a certain kind of clay. Sometimes homesick Dixie dirt-eaters exiled to the North would request that family members ship them a little bit of home sweet home—for supper.

Modern Southerners play down that sort of living off the land. I once asked a Mississippi man if lying down in the road and eating dirt were Southern customs. "I've never known anybody to eat dirt or nap in the road," he said, "but you might say that lying down is the most Southern custom of all."

Like lollygagging and hogging the remote control, cooking qualifies as a manly pastime in Dixie. The Southern chef stays with a meal from start to finish. He grows the vegetables, shoots the meat, and then mixes up his own secret sauce to smother them both. Since bringing home the bacon often comes under the heading "man's work," the stew pot or the skillet becomes the final stop on every hunting trip. The Dixie boy's all-time favorite recipes involve throwing on the fire what he's personally sent on to the Great Beyond. He performs a ritual postmortem, battering and frying and drowning in gravy that which once lived.

Still, the he-man Betty Crocker won't Ginsu just anything. Don't bother asking him to pickle okra or put up peach preserves; he has no patience for that stuff. He refuses to toss salad, and he'll have no part of a dessert-in-the-making, until it comes time to lick the bowl. And there's one kitchen task universally guaranteed to make the manly cook flee the scene: the clean-up. No matter what culinary gifts he displays during the preprandial preparations, after supper that son of a gun is vapor. Carv-

THINGS GO BETTER

G OOD OLD BOYS discovered early on that things go better with Coke. A shot of the elixir took the edge off the morning after. In what may have originally been a vain attempt to cheat the Devil, drinking men mixed the hangover remedy with the hangover cause hoping to preempt the day-after malaise.

Even without a liberal splash of whiskey added, however, Coke acquired a mildly sinful reputation in the early days when cocaine was rumored included among its ingredients. Church-going Southerners believed the soft drink tasted too good, so wickedly sweet that it certainly must be evil. But by the 1930s, a fellow could buy a Coke at a drugstore counter almost anywhere in the South. By 1950 he could get it anywhere in the world. Today it's not unusual to find Good Old Boys drinking Coke for breakfast or in the midafternoon in much the same way Germans gather for a beer or the Brits break for tea.

A BRIEF HISTORY OF SOUTHERN MANHOOD, continues

BLUEPRINT FOR DISASTER

THE BASIC INGREDIENTS in a simple Southern sour-mash whiskey are cornmeal, sugar, water, yeast, and malt, with embalming fluid and lye to add flavor optional. Each fifty-gallon batch yields about five gallons of drinking stock, which should be filtered through charcoal twice to minimize the headache poisons. Should be filtered, but often isn't. Sometimes the impatient dipsomaniac can't wait for moonshine to filter any more than a preschooler with a sweet tooth can wait for homemade cookies to cool. The result can hurt a dang sight worse than scorched fingers.

ing out a deer's entrails doesn't bother him in the least, but sticking his hands in dirty dishwater sure enough makes him queasy.

While the Good Old Boy gets the grease popping in the kitchen, the Southern Gentleman rattles ice cubes at the bar. To the Dixie-trained tippler, proper imbibing has nothing to do with the amount consumed and everything to do with the ritual accompanying the consumption. The regional rule is that a Southern man who can't hold his liquor should at least be able to pour it correctly and drink it with a little bit of style.

A friend told me a story about how her dad learned to drink. Seems a string of debaucheries, along with chronic truancy, landed him in trouble at college. So, his family packed him away to Virginia for a cure. They hoped that a semester or two under the aegis of a stern aunt there would rein in Sonny Boy's wildness.

This widowed aunt, a wise Southern belle of the steel magnolia variety, got to the root of her nephew's problem right away. The boy did not know how to drink properly. She went right to work on him. He learned "neat" from "straight up," and VS cognac from VSOP. One lesson dealt with swishing and sniffing brandy in a snifter. Another session taught him what every Southern man should know about juleps and planter's punch. This boy blazed through his aunt's customized curriculum faster than Sherman through Georgia. The topic held his interest. Once he'd mastered the subtleties of happy hour, he applied himself to his studies.

Male Southern drinkers halfway think fruity blender drinks garnished with umbrellas or sparklers call their manhood into question.

Before the Civil War, wine was hard to find in most areas of the South, and beer didn't get big down here until after refrigeration took hold. Serving whiskey has never been risky.

Time was when Southern men and women lined up on opposite sides of the temperance debate. I heard about a man in North Carolina whose wife frowned upon his occasional nip. To outsmart her, he poured his whiskey into a Coke bottle and hid it at various, convenient places around the house. Invariably, the old girl would discover his stash, empty the firewater, and replace it with soda pop. She played Eliot Ness to his Al Capone. And their little game of hide-and-seek continued, without mention, for more than forty years.

The hard-drinking Southern Gentleman works his elbow and his liver overtime, but the Good Old Boy gets powerful thirsty too. Necessity, they say, is the mother of invention, and the Good Old Boy has mastered the potluck happy hour. "Ever tried a Ray Charles cocktail?" a Good Old Boy with a hangover asked a friend early one morning. "It's black coffee, sugar, and gin. That's how Ray gets his voice to sound that way." Another favorite seat-of-the-pants concoction is bluesman John Lee Hooker's unique take on the boilermaker—one shot of bourbon, one shot of Scotch, and a beer.

During the do-dah days of the booming oil business in Texas and Louisiana, my brother—then a scrawny teenager—landed himself a summer job on a boat doing geological surveys in the Gulf of Mexico. On the second day at sea, his more seasoned colleagues began discussing something called

"the Green Goddess" in a lecherous tone not usually associated with talk about a salad dressing. My brother, green himself, assumed the goddess to be a famous prostitute working their next port of call.

Finally, late one night, the men declared that the hour of the Green Goddess drew nigh. As my brother tells it, his palms started sweating. The crew chief dimmed the ship's lights. The cook solemnly emerged from the galley carrying a liter bottle of Mountain Dew. The skipper brought forth a half-gallon jug of NyQuil, the alcohol-laced cold remedy. Mixed and served over ice, the Mountain Dew and NyQuil made a Green Goddess cocktail, the favored liqueur of resourceful Southern crewmen working in an environment mandated alcohol free. "If you're watching your weight," my brother says, "you could substitute Fresca."

I know an older Southern man who up and moved when his county went dry. You can imagine how upset he must have been during Prohibition. That officially booze-free decade rates right up there near the Civil War for unpleasantness as far as the South is concerned. A few Dixie boys managed to pull through by making crude wine or brewed beer at home. Chicken-fried logic dictated to many, however, that if a fellow was going to trouble himself with an illegal hooch operation, he might as well cook up something a good bit stronger than grape juice or a yeasty cocktail.

That something? Moonshine. Bust-head. Rotgut. Ruckus juice. White lightning. It puts hair on the chest, lead in the pencil. At 100 proof and sometimes more, Southern moonshine kicks like a mule. It looks clear, tastes raw, and sells fast even today.

Store-bought Southern whiskey slides down considerably smoother than the throat-searing homemade stuff. But even fine sipping stock like Jack Daniel's can leave its mark on a man. That's why a Southerner invented Coca-Cola, "the holy water of the American South," as a hangover cure.

At Darlington, South Carolina—the Mecca of stock-car racing—the public address announcer calls Coke "the special specialty" of the track. Well, if Co'Cola is this region's special specialty, iced tea (pronounced *ice* tea, the d is silent)—is the house wine, as long it's served with mint, lemon, and enough sugar to rot your teeth. Down here only foreigners and sick people drink hot tea.

A Southern scholar irked by what he deemed factual errors in the film *Mississippi Burning* pointed to one glaring mistake: "Y'all know the scene where the FBI guy goes to the woman's house and she offers him iced tea? Well, she asks if he'd like it sweetened or unsweetened! No self-respecting Southerner would ever ask that."

Traditionally Southerners eat big at lunchtime and call it "dinner." In the years before air-conditioning altered almost every aspect of Southern life, a fellow escaped the heat by taking a short nap beneath the whirring ceiling fan on his sleeping porch after dinner. These days, by the time a working man commutes back out to the pine and Bermuda grass suburbs for lunch, he barely has time to nuke a cup o' soup or mug o' pizza before it's time to hit the highway again.

I encountered a Good Old Boy bemoaning the demise of the old ways of Southern eating. "When I was a boy, we ate in shifts because there wasn't room for everybody at the table all at once. The men ate first, the women ate second, and the kids got whatever was left. Now it seems like the whole society has changed. With all this women's lib stuff, the women eat first, then the children, then the men. Know what that means? I ate last according to the old rules, and I eat last by the new rules. Doesn't seem fair."

My mama once advised me that before ever telling a man bad news, I should always feed him first. "You want to know what men like?" Mama asked. "The smell of chicken frying." I think she might be right. Sex scientists figured out a few years ago that the average American man thinks about you-know-what every fifteen seconds or so. I'll go dollars to doughnuts that every sixteenth second, the average Southern man fantasizes about food. By the count of seventeen, he's probably considering getting drunk, which brings him right back around to sex again.

Food comes up there close to football and Jesus on the Southern man's hierarchy of values. Food speaks a language all its own. Gifts of food are an offering of heart and soul. At a "sitting up," or funeral wake, Southern mourners offer condolences with casseroles. Southern men use sweets to say "Hey, honey, how's about me 'n' you?" and they eat massive quantities of heart-stopping calories to assert their masculinity in an I-dare-this-pig-to-kill-me sort of way.

A Southern Gentleman I know one day suspected that his wife and his best friend had run off to New Orleans for an illicit meeting. In a fit of rage, he tracked them down at a French Quarter hotel. Rather than knock on their love-nest door unprepared to even the score, he decided that he'd go home, fetch his gun, come back, and kill them both. On his way, he stopped at Cafe du Monde for coffee and beignets. There, good food and a cool river breeze calmed him down and changed his mind.

Such is the power of Southern cooking. They call it soul food because it fires as well as soothes the soul.

CHAPTER FOUR

White Bucks & Red Necks

Sansabelt Haute Couture

T HERE ARE PRECIOUS FEW THINGS IN LIFE that a belle can count on. The phone ringing as soon as she gets in the shower. Her slip showing during only the most important job interviews. And the way the men in her life throw together an outfit.

In case you hadn't noticed, Southern men lag about ten years behind the fashion vanguard. If a Southern Gentleman slips his britches on backward, he's not trying for a hip-hop look. He's drunk. And when a Good Old Boy shows up at a party wearing a plaid flannel shirt and steel-toed boots, he's not going for "grunge." He just got off from work. Menswear designers might be showing parachute pants with pleats this season, but most Southern boys couldn't care less. They buy new clothes only when the old ones blow out—and sometimes not even then.

The polo pony or that family crest thing might be the trendy pocket logo of the moment in some places, but the only monogram the authentic Southern Gentleman really takes a shine to is his own. And even then, he likes it hidden discreetly on the cuff or on the shirttail for the benefit of the laundry. Those initials also happened to belong to his father and his grandfather, which makes it so much easier to wear hand-me-downs. As one natty secondhand Southerner said, "Why else you think they named me John, Jr.?"

Preworns form a fair chunk of most Southern wardrobes, but the idea of paying extra for "distressed" khakis makes the Dixie boy sick to his stomach. "Let me get this straight: It's used, so I'm paying double?" A stylish hunk in Manhattan or L.A. might have no problem strutting around in a leather motorcycle jacket covered with metal hardware, but the studly Southerner rebel goes for something more functional. A plain denim jacket, for instance, keeps him warm, won't set off airport security alarms, and carries a price tag that leaves beer money in his pocket.

The Southern man's top fashion watchwords? "Comfortable" and "traditional." Two terms with no place in his sartorial vernacular? "Cutting edge" and "Euro-styling." Come to think of it, the closets of heterosexual Southern males could well represent the graveyard of all fashion trends. These guys don't dress to please women. They pull their pants on one leg at time, and they select those polyesters to suit nobody but them-

THE FRONT PORCH:
Ugly

"*IF YOU CAN'T be beautiful you might as well be smart,*" *Southern mothers teach belles-in-training. Southern boys hear the same tutorial, in reverse. Pretty, for a man, is a sorry consolation prize, but a Southern woman can barely get a driver's license without it.*

If a girl grows up plain, she'd better be charming. An unattractive man, on the other hand, wears his warts as a badge of masculinity. The Southern man actually values ugly. How else to explain why the Good Old Boys of the world started to respect Elvis only once the King got fat?

To Dixie Boys, ugly means scrappy. As in "How 'bout them ugly Bulldogs!" when Georgia beats up on a prettier team. Ugly means macho. As in "Honey, you wait here. It might get ugly in there." But sometimes, Southern ugly still translates simply as the flip side of beautiful.

The Southern man gets on the terminology of hideousness like ugly on an ape. "Homemade sin," while more severe than "mud fence" but not as heinous as "clock stopping," has been used as benchmark ugly for years. "Rawboned" pretty much says it too, as does "fell out of the ugly tree." A buck-toothed ugly person could "bite a hog through a picket fence." A skinny, homely type might be able to "take a bath in a gun barrel."

Ugly discriminates. When a fellow describes an amply proportioned woman as "fat as a town cow," he's not sweet-talking her. But make no mistake: If he says of a man, "When that guy hauls ass, he has to make two trips," it's high flattery. Sort of like "bad" equals "good" to boys in the hood, "ugly" means "admirable" to boys in the woods.

A BRIEF HISTORY OF SOUTHERN MANHOOD, continues

selves—obviously. Down here, the clothes don't make the man. The man makes the man. The clothes just let you know he's Southern.

But what kind of Southern? A girl wondering whether she's sitting across the table from a Good Old Boy or a Southern Gentleman should just take a gander at his necktie. A clip-on hollers Good Old Boy. A silk stripe indicates Gentleman.

To the Good Old Boy "good grooming" means cleaning his finger-nails with his pocketknife and picking his teeth with the corner of a matchbook cover after a big meal. He smells like Brut cologne. He wears a short crew cut, with little bumps on the back of his neck from the bar-ber's shears. His socks gleam, always white. His face shines as red as a tom turkey's neck, thanks to cheap bourbon and ample Southern sun-shine. When the advertisement on his gimme cap matches the company name on his golf shirt, he feels dapper and has probably expended more than a little effort coordinating his ensemble.

Unlike the Good Old Boy, the Southern Gentleman splashes on imported Bay Rum after a shave. Instead of the Good Old Boy's signature comb tracks through a well-oiled crew cut, the dashing Southern Gen-tleman fancies his hair a little longer, but not *too* long. The hat he doffs is more likely a straw boater than a mesh gimme. He might sport a bow tie and suspenders at the office, and on weekends he dresses as much like an Ivy League prepster as possible. If his button-down shirts are frayed at the cuffs, or his khakis have gone threadbare in the seat, so much the bet-ter. In screwy places like Hollywood, a man might send his trusty blue blazer to the Salvation Army when the lapel width goes out of style, but not the Southern Gentleman. He'll keep it and wear it until the cut comes in and goes out of style again and again and again.

If you've never been shopping with a Good Old Boy, you're missing something that rates right up there with frog gigging. When he shops, which is rarely, he heads to Wal-Mart. He gets his automotive supplies there. At the worm bar, he browses for neon fishing lures, "bait à la carte." He throws a garden hose plus twenty feet of rope into his shopping cart just because

101 USES FOR KUDZU
#23—Snake motel.

A BRIEF HISTORY OF SOUTHERN MANHOOD, continues

those two items always come in handy. And beneath that unambiguous MEN banner behind housewares, he updates his wardrobe. He selects a couple of pairs of the ever-popular tube socks in superabsorbent white cotton. A zip-up jumpsuit—the classic puttering uniform now in new back-to-nature colors—might call out to him. Without even so much as leaning toward the fitting room, he chooses a size 46 husky X-tra long with a self-belt and kingly patch logo above the breast pocket.

If the Good Old Boy feels jaunty, on top of his game, he might decide he deserves something special. Throw caution to the wind. He's going all the way. "Why not be good to myself? I've earned it!" He plucks a plump three-pack of Fruit of the Looms from a merry-go-round sales rack and calls her a done deal. From the underwear department he saunters straight on over to HARDWARE. Through the years, Southern women have learned to respect the efficiency, if not the style, of a man who buys his underwear and power tools at the same time.

Farmers still favor overalls as functional fashion. A good percentage of the male retirees in Dixie might be tempted to walk right up and kiss the genius designer who first adapted the fighter pilot's flight jumper as suburban lawn wear. My next-door neighbor zips one on every morning of the year before he strolls outside to begin his day's work—accosting joggers with his World War II stories and occasionally watering the lawn.

All work and no play would, in theory, make Jim Buddy a dull boy. But if you know a Jim Buddy, you understand that there's no reason to worry. He plays plenty. Even his weekend wear makes a certain rebel fashion statement. Appropriate for work or play, the ubiquitous "white trash tuxedo"—blue jeans, white shirt,

SMELLS LIKE MACHO SPIRIT

Aqua-Velva
Brut
Hickory smoke
Old Spice
Hai Karate
Beer
Gym socks
Catfish Charlie
Bay Rum
Bourbon

sports jacket (never called just a "jacket" or "blazer" in Dixie)—takes the hick on the go from daytime into evening; from the construction site to the monster-truck rally as the case may be. And belles have come to love this look. Burt Reynolds made it sexy in the 1970s, and Billy Ray Cyrus keeps the faith today.

Then there's that whole school of Good-Old-Boy casual, which involves adapting golf wear for everywhere wear. Loud golf pants, in colors bright enough to make your fillings hurt, sum up the Southerner's idea of kick-ass casual for those days he uses "party" as a verb. Golf connotes leisure down South, and free time brings to mind images of kingly grandeur. The Good Old Boy believes a golf shirt allows him to outsmart dress codes requiring a necktie. In some way he thinks golf wear, even cheap golf wear, affords him a Palm Beach look and gives him the right to a privileged, man-of-means swagger. Jim Buddy figures that bright-green slacks and a plaid Johnny Carson sports jacket will go anywhere—dress it up for a Rotarians luncheon, or dress it down for a domino game at the Am Vets hall. And if the golf-casual Good Old Boy so happens to find himself near the links with an hour or so to kill, he can always spank a round.

Some daring Southern men will attempt wearing jewelry from time to time—a big chunky gold Rolex, or a manly diamond ring. But for the most part, Dixie boys find such baubles disturbing. "Ten-to-one says a guy wearing a diamond ring has got his net worth sitting on his finger. And I'll go you double or nothing that he beats his wife."

The ultimate Good-Old-Boy fashion accessory isn't gold. It's flesh—the trophy gut. He flops it over his belt as a badge of honor. He rubs it. Bounces it like a basketball. Kneads it like Play-doh. Stroking his splendid spare tire with pride, he frequently asks half rhetorically: "Don't you wish you had one like this?" His ever-present pal acts as a buffer, or a bumper, between him and the rest of the world.

HICK HAIR

- **The Porter Wagoner**—requires more hairspray than they use on Dolly Parton's wig.
- **The Jimmy Swaggart**—a born-again pompadour.
- **Carolina Comb Tracks**—a sure sign of bad breeding.
- **El Camino**—two hairdos on one head; short in front, long in back.
- **The Porcupine**—Bill Clinton wears it well.
- **The Hair Hat**—a removable Burt Reynolds special.

A BRIEF HISTORY OF SOUTHERN MANHOOD, continues

1897 New Orleans' Storyville becomes a legal red-light district.

Unaware of proper belly etiquette, I embarrassed myself once at a Southern wedding. The father of the bride approached me, threw his arm around my shoulder, and directed my gaze down to the majestic stomach pushing his necktie straight out, parallel to the ground. "Have you ever seen one like this before?" he asked, beaming.

"Not outside a circus," I responded a little bit too quickly. Prying my eyes away from this *Guinness Book* gullet, I looked at the man's face and saw that I had delivered a body blow. He'd sought a few kind words for his friend and gotten a cruel jab right smack in the breadbasket.

Somewhere I read that on average, American women subtract about two pounds when they give their weight. Good Old Boys *add* poundage. Holding tight to the theory that weight equals power and power equals sex appeal, big-bellied Southern men like to peel off their shirts. They unveil a big stomach at the slightest provocation, and defend it: "I'm not a trail-mix kinda guy. I don't do sprouts. Y'all think I could have built a jewel like this out of lettuce?"

At a University of Tennessee football game, a full-figured Good Old Boy noticed several topless, flat-bellied younger men standing side by side. Each man had one letter painted on his washboard stomach, and together they spelled out VOLS, the name of their team. "Vols, my hind foot!" the great-gutted one said. "I could write University of Tennessee Volunteers across my belly alone."

Not all Southern men strut the physiques of sumo wrestlers, of

HE SAYS "DAPPER"; SHE SAYS "REPULSIVE"

- **Clip-on suspenders:** The braces that button inside the waistbands of well-tailored suits aren't so bad as long the dollar-sign or naked-lady logo isn't excessively obnoxious. But the clip-ons? The ones Mork from Ork wore? The perennial fashion favorites with pimply-faced kids at fast-food counters? Those babies have no place in a grown man's wardrobe.
- **Speedo swimsuits:** "Banana slings" or "teeny weenie bikinis" are ten times yukkier to the average Southern belle than even the most thoroughly shot Jockey shorts.
- **Tightie whitie Jockey shorts:** The ones that look great on Jim Palmer look disgusting on a man with a big belly. And the bigger his middle, the more likely a man seems to cling to a pair of BVDs until they turn dingy gray and go so threadbare as to become transparent.
- **Vinyl shoes:** There must be something wrong with the Good Old Boy's eyesight if he thinks they come close to passing for leather even from ten yards away.

A BRIEF HISTORY OF SOUTHERN MANHOOD, continues

course. If the Good Old Boy carries too much pork under his shirt, the Gentleman totes too little. And the only time he willingly goes shopping for new clothes is when the little heft he does have redistributes.

When forced by nature to update his wardrobe, the Gentleman spends a whole day at Brooks Brothers. There he buys a summer or a winter suit, six white shirts, three silk neckties, new khakis, and a dozen pairs of plain white boxer shorts. He makes fashion choices that guarantee he won't stand out in his fraternity's group photo.

I heard a story about an outdoor wedding in Virginia, where all the groomsmen were instructed to wear blue blazers, bow ties, and khaki pants. On the day of the ceremony, the photographer found it difficult to separate the members of the wedding party from the other male guests who all wore some slight variation of the same outfit.

The Southern Gentleman feels most comfortable in a uniform that remains as timeless and reassuring as Robert E. Lee's gray and gold. I'm talking seersucker, of course. If the Good Old Boy has made the trophy gut his trademark, the Gentleman has registered the seersucker suit.

One hot and sticky Sunday morning after church, I watched one big Detroit land yacht after another pull into the dusty parking lot of the country club in Clarksdale, Mississippi. Inside, where everybody lined up at the steam table to heap plates full of fried chicken, roughly 90 percent of the males—from doddering grandpas to rambunctious toddlers—wore some version of the official summertime suit of the South.

Despite what you may have heard late-night comedians say, seersucker does not refer to the sucking sound of bare legs separating from a Naugahyde sofa on a searing Southern day. It comes from the Persian *shir o shakkar,* which means "milk and sugar," and refers to the plain and

BUMPER STICKER

CLEAN UP THE SOUTH:
BUY A YANKEE A BUS TICKET.

1900   The word "hillbilly" first appears in print referring to a "free and untrammeled white citizen of Alabama, who lives in the hills, has no means to speak of, dresses as he can, talks as he pleases, drinks whiskey when he gets it, and fires off his revolver as the fancy takes him."   **55**

puckered stripes. They invented the stuff in India, where the colonial Brits got hip to it as the best way this side of buck naked to beat the tropical heat.

In some areas of the United States, seersucker underlines "I'm from out of town" even more than a Carolina accent. A Southern Gentleman riding a bus through a bad neighborhood in Manhattan worried that his seersucker suit made him a more attractive target for muggers. "I didn't dare open my mouth," he said. "Just in case some of them hadn't already figured out where I was from."

Seersucker never needs ironing, and doesn't ever go out of style or season in Dixie. It's a front porch suit, a verandah look, something a fellow never wears for long without a cool drink in his hand. Your grandpa probably owned a seersucker suit. When my grandpa's arthritis got so bad he couldn't negotiate a zipper, he had Velcro sewn into the fly of his seersucker, saying "This is really the only suit a man like me needs." He wore it practically every day.

Bible salesmen foraging around the Delta

NON-SOUTHERNERS WHO COULD PASS FOR DIXIE BOYS

Nikita Khrushchev
John Candy
Joe Namath
John Wayne
John Goodman
Boris Yeltsin
Tim Allen
Ernest Hemingway
Rush Limbaugh
Tom Arnold
Sumo wrestlers
Rodney Dangerfield

A BRIEF HISTORY OF SOUTHERN MANHOOD, continues

1902 Willis Haviland Carrier invents air-conditioning.

backwater pushing the Word on widow women favor seersucker because it travels so well. And just about every Southern politician since the carpetbaggers headed home has relied on seersucker stripes to convey "man of the people," whether he fits that bill or not. Gregory Peck in *To Kill a Mockingbird* might deserve credit for making seersucker seem sexy. An older belle told me that she digs Andy Griffith's seersucker on *Matlock*. And Nick Nolte never looked tastier than he did as the square-but-sexy, seersuckered South Carolinian in *Prince of Tides,* and as the natty North Carolina lawyer in *Cape Fear.*

Not just any old seersucker will do. "The stripes really should be gray and white," said a suit salesman in New Orleans. "Blue is okay for some people, I guess. Green, I wouldn't recommend wearing around here. And the multicolored stripes are just, well, they're just un-Christian."

Ages before the first rapper busted a rhyme and worn-backward droopy jeans became the rage, the Southern Gentleman was telling his tailor to cut his seersuckers extra roomy. How come? Because someone, somewhere down South started the rumor long ago that tight trousers were for sissies. Besides baggy seersucker, Gentlemen go big for roomy khakis, not denim. Good Old Boys, on the other hand, think baggy pants seem fruity. So skin-tight denim works just fine for them as long as it's not acid washed. "Now, that really *is* for sissies."

There was a time when you could play "find the Volvo" in Dixie and win with a score of two. Same with "spy the Armani." But even back then, there lurked a certain type of Southerner the other boys suspected might care a little too much about style.

You probably know such a slave to fashion. You maybe dated him, or even married him. He has good luck with women, and it drives the other guys absolutely crazy. They can't for the life of them figure out his chick magnetism. He's got quite a flair for fashion and sometimes veers dangerously near the fruit bowl. He knows he's playing with fire. So he takes care to talk extra football just in case some of the Good Old Boys find out about his *GQ* subscription and go getting the wrong idea.

Then there are those Southern men who enjoy dressing up. A friend told me a story about her cousin, a trend-setting fop who finished Vanderbilt last year and spent the summer with his family in North Carolina. On Easter afternoon, he came downstairs wearing a pair of pleated white trousers with tiny blue pinstripes and a pale-blue shirt. To this he had added a bow tie, some suspenders, and a 1930s, Huey Long–style straw hat. He carried a copy of *The Great Gatsby*, as sort of a prop, to finish off his look.

The young gadfly breezed into the family room. His father, dressed in the usual early country-club ensemble, roared with laughter. His brother, clad in Bermudas and T-shirt, hit him with a rolled-up magazine and said, "Have you gone totally light in your loafers? Get upstairs and take off that dang costume before we're all the talk of the town."

Sons of the South want nothing so much as to be swashbuckling. Women love men in uniform; it's true. But not nearly as much as men love being in uniform. When I was in college, each spring the Southern Gentlemen of Kappa Alpha fraternity would put on Confederate military regalia and go calling at sorority houses—sometimes on horseback. At each house, the gentlemen hand-delivered formal invitations to their annual Old South ball. Once the bids had been doled out, the brothers got good and drunk and threw laundry soap in the campus fountain, or stole a statue of the university founder. Maybe red-blooded Southern boys can sustain perfect drawing-room manners for only so long before they feel compelled to run outside, have a snort, and emit blood-curdling Rebel yells. These reassuring rituals must somehow remind them who wears the pants in Dixie.

Or who doesn't. I heard about a distinguished Garden District gentleman who became bored with trousers. So he started dressing each morning in a pink shirt, bow tie, starched white lab coat with a carnation in the lapel, black socks, and wing tips—no britches. Eccentric? Maybe a little bit. But he took pride in his appearance, and spent time developing his signature style. I know of a Delta doctor who likes to dress up in medieval knight's wear as a hobby. A friend in Mississippi hung a photograph of himself wearing a Confederate military uniform as king of the Natchez pageant in his study. And then there's the construction contractor in Texas who dabbles in local politics and also enjoys wearing ladies' chiffon evening gowns.

Men who play dress up: fetish or fashion?

It sounds almost like a *Donahue* topic, but a friend, engaged for the second time around, lived it.

Divorced, in her mid-thirties, my friend became reacquainted with a man she had not seen since high school. She knew his family; he knew hers. They had many friends in common. When they reconnected, both recently untethered, the two fell instantly in love and made plans to marry.

One night after dinner, about a week before the wedding, the groom dropped a bombshell on his intended. "Darlin'," he drawled, "I'd like to share something with you that I've never shared with another living soul."

Not sure exactly what to say, she nodded, halfway scared. He excused himself and dashed upstairs promising to be right back.

While she waited, the belle flipped through several cable channels, nagged by the memory of a story she'd read in the tabloids about a man who told his fiancée on their wedding night that he was a transvestite and then asked to borrow her black half slip. Finally my friend clicked off the television and poured herself a bourbon. That way, just in case her beloved came down the stairs dressed as Ethel Merman, she'd be fortified.

After she'd thrown back two little shots of distilled composure, her beau returned bedecked in full Confederate regalia—gray uniform, sash, saber, the whole show. Solemnly removing his hat, he bowed gallantly and introduced himself as Colonel William Littlejohn. Then he proceeded to recite a pretty decent poem he'd written about love, death, and lessons learned from war. He sat there until midnight, spinning this fiction with a totally straight face.

The next morning the colonel had vanished. My friend's fiancé, dressed in his regular twentieth-century clothes, shoveled down grits and gulped coffee as if nothing had ever happened. He was once again an average Southern suit-and-tie rack.

The newest living Confederate bride tells all: "It's almost like I married a cross-dresser. The weirdest part is, I kind of like it."

CHAPTER FIVE

Taking a Load Off

Football, Noodling for Catfish
& Spanking a Round of Golf

"**M**ABEL, HOLD MY CALLS. AND BRING ME some Alka-Seltzer."

Not long ago I saw an item in the newspaper about a distinguished banking executive in Charlotte, North Carolina, who took a break from his hectic schedule to glue 216 antacid tablets to his body.

Sound like a moron with an upset stomach? Guess again. Our Mr. High Finance had more than a heartburn; he had himself a plan. Once he had slipped into his seltzer suit, he waltzed right outside and went for a dip in a downtown reflecting pool. As the fountain fizzed, the effervescent banker bounced out of the water, punched the air, and shouted: "Carolina Panthers!"

The Carolina Panthers hadn't played a single game. They weren't even a team at the time. This sports fan wasted all that antacid relief just to show how passionately *he would* support those Panthers should the NFL choose to park an expansion franchise in Charlotte. Another local businessman dressed up in a gorilla suit and monkeyed through a busy mall to further emphasize his city's unmatched enthusiasm for football.

Charlotte got the franchise. But to be crazier about football than other Southern cities? Well, that's saying a lot. When a Texas high-school team lost a game 37–0, the school board president went after the coach with a knife. The residents of Troy, Texas (population 1,390), voted to change the name of their town to Troy Aikman, Texas, in honor of the beloved Dallas Cowboys' quarterback. All over this region, folks get plain silly about watching grown men push the pigskin around the pasture. But the Southern male gets pretty fired up about stock-car racing and golf and hunting and fishing and wrestling and all things not work-related. When God made weekends, he had the Dixie boy in mind.

To watch a Southern man relax is like seeing Baryshnikov dance or hearing Pavarotti sing. Any woman lucky enough to witness the poetry of a Dixie rascal in full repose knows she's seeing Rembrandt at the easel.

The Southerner lounges actively, and never haphazardly. There's order and reason behind his well-honed slothfulness, rigid rules of relaxation that he does his damnedest to stick to. First, he's wrapped his IQ around the idea that a man must spend his considerable spare time engaged in manly pursuits. You know, things like killing animals and

THE FRONT PORCH:
Visiting

IF HE'S NOT sawing off a whopper or spinning a windy, he's likely listening to another fellow jaw. Visiting can stir up a right refreshing breeze on hot summer afternoons below the Mason-Dixon.

Around here, the verbs "to visit" and "to talk" are practically interchangeable. The South stays about half drunk on its own potent, home-brewed mythology. An advertisement for cheap long-distance rates summed it up: "Visiting is a favorite pastime in the South. Southerners love to talk. . . . This Saturday, swap stories. Share a secret. Visit with your folks. It's a custom worth keeping."

And is it ever kept! Southerners dial up a wrong number and talk for an hour. The Dixie boy blows long and hard about Mama, Daddy, the War, and the grandeur of days gone by. When there's nobody around to listen to him yak, he might ask himself a question, wait a few minutes, and then answer it. He's not crazy. He's just keeping his visitation skills sharp.

Really gifted Southern storytellers can make even the dullest tale entertaining. A popular Southern yarn has to do with a group of men visiting around a campfire on a hunting trip. One smooth-talker among them would shout, "Number three," and all the other guys would bust a gut laughing. A newcomer in the circle thought he'd give it a whirl. He hollered, "Number four," and a sudden silence fell over the gathering. Finally one of the old-timers put a friendly hand on the greenhorn's shoulder and said, "Don't worry. Some can tell 'em, some can't."

A BRIEF HISTORY OF SOUTHERN MANHOOD, continues

MUSIC HE LIKES . . .

Creedence Clearwater
Lynyrd Skynyrd
The Allman Brothers
B.B. King
Elvis
Reba McEntire
R.E.M.
Hank Williams, Jr.
Muddy Waters
Tom T. Hall
Dolly Parton
Clifton Chenier
ZZ Top
Aretha Franklin
Vern Gosdin

MUSIC HE DOESN'T . . .

Opera
Rap
Yanni
Yoko Ono
Michael Bolton
Axel Rose

looking at monster-truck rallies on the TV. He thinks "culture" is about half effeminate. Going to a ballet or an opera is something a fellow's wife makes him do. That's okay for some wimps, the Dixie boy believes, but not for him. No siree. He doesn't hover around women day and night letting them run his life. "Do I, honey?"

A second important aspect of a man's leisure requires the exclusion of women. Tennis, aerobics, power walking—"Shoot! That's girl stuff." The moment a woman takes an interest in a hobby, it becomes instantly unacceptable to the Southern male. A man's avocation must exclude women, and it must *include* other men. Boys were bonding in the woods of Dixie long before New Age fellows dreamed up drumming and sweat lodges. Remembrances of military glory, fraternity pranks, field-house frolics never fail to bring a sparkle to the Southern boy's eyes.

The South has risen again, all right, on the playing field. When a Southern athlete or team marches north, east, or west, they're not just headed

101 USES FOR KUDZU
#71—Car cover.

A BRIEF HISTORY OF SOUTHERN MANHOOD, continues

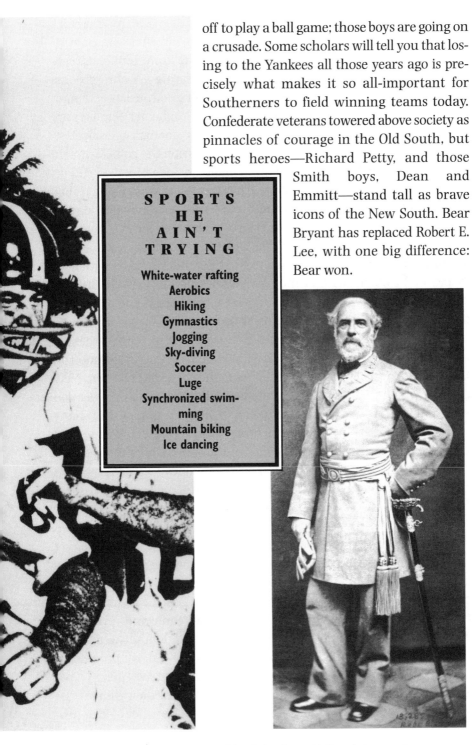

off to play a ball game; those boys are going on a crusade. Some scholars will tell you that losing to the Yankees all those years ago is precisely what makes it so all-important for Southerners to field winning teams today. Confederate veterans towered above society as pinnacles of courage in the Old South, but sports heroes—Richard Petty, and those Smith boys, Dean and Emmitt—stand tall as brave icons of the New South. Bear Bryant has replaced Robert E. Lee, with one big difference: Bear won.

SPORTS HE AIN'T TRYING

White-water rafting
Aerobics
Hiking
Gymnastics
Jogging
Sky-diving
Soccer
Luge
Synchronized swimming
Mountain biking
Ice dancing

1916   Stone Mountain in Georgia dedicated as a memorial to the Lost Cause with Mount Rushmore—style sculptures of Robert E. Lee, Jefferson Davis, and Stonewall Jackson.

"The Good Lord Jesus gave us the Word, and the Word was football." When folks say that the most popular religions in Dixie are Baptist, Methodist, and Football, they're semiserious. The Protestant congregations require the baptism of the faithful, but bearing a Y chromosome serves as sufficient initiation into the covenant of gridiron action. A man who doesn't "observe" carries the stigma of a blasphemer. Sundays are for kicking butt and saving souls down here where football and salvation are sometimes synonyms. The Southern fan sees nothing coincidental in the fact that his most sacred religious holidays include a football ritual.

Football can heal like a TV preacher too. All those racial tensions simmering below the surface of Southern society cool on game day, as black and white fans implore: "We'll love one another for four quarters, Jesus. Just please, oh, please, let the Bulldogs beat the bookie's line." It's not unusual for a man of the cloth to end his Sunday sermon with a little prayer for the triumph of the Cowboys or Oilers or Falcons. Still not convinced? In New Orleans, the Southern capital of sin and bacchanalian debauchery, they call their team "The Saints."

If professional football is like a Wednesday night prayer meeting, college football is high mass. A bowl game roughly equals the Sermon on the Mount. Loyal alums elevate coaches to the status of holy men. Never mind what professorial types say about athletics being to education what bullfighting is to agriculture. That's just sour grapes. Not many professors get fan letters, or have an honor guard of state troopers escort them to work like Coach Vince Dooley of the University of Georgia did. Of Bear Bryant, the holiest of coaching clerics, one of his congregation reportedly once said, "He could have gotten himself elected governor, if he'd wanted to lower himself to that level."

A popular artifact in Tuscaloosa was a portrait of Bear walking on water. When the gridiron god died, one follower suggested that grief got him. Sadness over never beating Notre Dame sent the great man to his grave. "He coached himself to death, that's what." Nearly fifteen hundred people showed up at his memorial service. That's a better turnout than Jefferson Davis drew. An additional ten thousand mourners, dressed in red-and-white Crimson Tide T-shirts, caps, and sweatshirts, lined the streets of downtown Tuscaloosa as the funeral procession passed. One banner of tribute read GOD NEEDS AN OFFENSIVE COORDINATOR. Southerners never doubt that the Almighty is a fan of their game.

And it is the South's game, at least that's the way the rabid Southern armchair quarterback sees it. One Joseph William Namath of Beaver Falls, Pennsylvania, noticed right off that Southerners have a peculiar proprietary relationship with the sport. When Joseph William started throwing touchdown passes in college at Alabama, he became "Joe Willie," and his "youse guys" changed to "y'all."

At Hampden–Sydney College in Virginia, Southern fans have combined two beloved sacraments—the football game and the cocktail party. While the team's quarterback flings Hail Marys on the field, spectators stand around on a grassy hill throwing back bloody Marys. Football the way the good Lord intended.

Football is universal. Neither the Southern Gentleman nor the Good Old Boy can pull himself away, but when it comes to other diversions they might differ on the best way to kill a Saturday afternoon. The only spectacle more heart-warming to a Good Old Boy than Alabama vs. Texas A & M at the Sugar Bowl is Richard Petty in the winner's circle at Darlington. The South's claim on football might be hard to truss up in an argument, but the Dixie boy can call stock-car racing homegrown without a challenge. That sport grew right out of the Southern landscape when the moonshiners of Wilkes County, North Carolina, souped up their Detroit hot rods to outrun the government revenuers. Good Old Boys see stock-car racing in much the same way Western ranch hands see rodeo: as an entertaining display of practical skill. It never hurts a cowboy to be agile with rope, and it never hurts a Dixie boy to be one step ahead of the authorities, just in case.

If the Devil showed up on the avid race fan's porch and offered him two tickets to Daytona in exchange for his soul, his wife's soul, and the souls of his children, the guts-on-floor race fan would say, "What's the catch?"

Along with watching skinny guys with mustaches drive flat out and belly to the ground, your average motor-sports devotee probably also digs bleached blond babes spilling silicone out of their push-up bras and Hank Williams, Jr.'s anthems about kicking butt. Fight hard, love long, drive fast—that's the Southern motor man's motto. Heck, it's his mantra.

If football and stock-car racing seem like

HEROES OF THE CLUTCH

Richard Petty
Davey Allison
Dale Earnhardt
Bill Elliot
David Pearson
Joe Weatherley
Fireball Roberts
Junior Johnson
Ned Jarrett
Tim Richmond

A BRIEF HISTORY OF SOUTHERN MANHOOD, continues

snug fits for the Good Old Boy's temperament, baseball chafes and itches. For the Good Old Boy, baseball isn't the national pastime, channel surfing through the summer is. All those weenies who write essays about baseball hearkening back to our agrarian past really get the Good Old Boy's bile ducts pumping. Agrarian past? The Good Old Boy experienced that agrarian past firsthand, and for the life of him he can't see the connection between farm chores and riding the pine sucking on sunflower seeds. The Good Old Boy likes to take his own sweet time in life, but baseball is *too* slow, swamp-turtle slow. Too many stats, too much talk, not enough bone crunching. And no good nicknames. "When Ted Turner fields a Braves team with guys named Boog, Big 'Un, and Skeeter, then we'll talk."

The Southern Gentleman has been talking baseball all his life. The game's leisurely pace and arcane facts captivate him. And while basketball isn't big in the Deep South, it rules on Tobacco Road with the Gentlemanly set. Season tickets to the Dean Dome in Chapel Hill are a hot commodity. Charles Barkley comes from Alabama, and Southerners like to remind folks that Michael Jordan was a superstar around here before anybody even thought of naming a sneaker after him.

The Good Old Boy could go either way on basketball. Watching all that running up and down, up and down might make his head swim and his eyeballs tired, but when a local team has a chance to snag an invite to the Big Dance, he'll pay attention. He'll root for the Blue Devils or the Tar Heels. It won't kill him to use the company's Hornets tickets a few times a year, but for the most part, the Good Old Boy likes his sport a little

1918 Cookies and marshmallow are combined to make the first Moon Pie at the Chattanooga Bakery in Tennessee.

more on the rowdy side. He'll tolerate ice hockey for just that reason. To his way of thinking, you have to love a game where a guy gets nothing but a few minutes in the corner for something that would draw hard time if done in the parking lot. "What's the fun in watching if there's not even a chance that somebody's going to get killed?"

Spectator sports should be full contact, but the games in which the Southern man will participate, well, that's a different story. The big fan will savor most anything with a televised play by play, but there's a long laundry list of sporting activities he'd never even consider trying. Jogging, for one. He might do it, if somebody was shooting at him or chasing him with a warrant. He retains some respect for Bill Clinton simply because Clinton seems to jog for the right reason—to get to those hot fries and factory-fresh Egg McMuffins down at Mickey D's. Otherwise, jogging just seems stupid. "If you're in a hurry, get in the damn car."

Skiing—water and snow—the Good Old Boy also avoids. He enjoyed the show at Cypress Gardens, and he owns a bass rig powerful enough to pull Lulu from *Hee Haw* across the wake on a slalom, but the Southern man himself would never be caught dead on a pair of skis. He can't stop thinking about water-skiing as being dragged by a speed boat and snow skiing as falling down a mountain with two-by-fours on your feet.

"Year-round golf," one transplanted Floridian says, "that's what I like about the South." Yeah, well, that's just what most Southerners don't like about migratory snowbirds—they clog up the links. Aside from the invading Northern hordes, so many things about golf seem tailor-made for the Southern sports enthusiast. He really warms up to the golf cart, for example. It allows him to consider himself an athlete without burning any calories. A man actually could put on weight playing golf, since he can drink and smoke and snack between shots. Betting can make golf profitable. Golf clothes show off the belly to its best advantage. And if done right, golf gives a man the chance to escape from women without having to go hole up in a cold, damp duck blind.

The Southern Gentleman prefers whacking his weekend round at a club where the rules keep ladies from teeing off until after noon, where waiters bring cool beer out to the tenth tee box, and where the men's grill is home to big business deals. Where the Good Old Boy swings his sticks, the rules don't keep women off the course nearly so much as the prospect of seeing fat guys sucking down malt liquor for breakfast does. At the Good Old Boy's municipal course there's not a men's grill, just a vending machine where he can nab some peanut butter cheese crackers and a Snickers for lunch.

Just when you start to think that his idea of athletic prowess is four shots at the nineteenth hole, or that he considers braving the elements to mean tolerating snow on the Magnavox, the Dixie boy might surprise you and suddenly go outside to play. That's the reason he stays on his back so much of time anyway, you know. He's storing up power for a hunting trip. He keeps his guns spic and span, boots in the truck, and dog panting by the door. When he hears the call of the wild, he answers on the first ring.

GONE NOODLIN'

THE SAME FOLKS who gave the world fishing with dynamite and who innovated techniques for telephoning supper out of the lake also bring you "noodling for catfish." No hooks, lines, or sinkers necessary, only a can of automotive grease. The sportsman lubes his arm up to the elbow to mask his human scent. Then he grabs the snoozing catfish from their mud beds at the bottom of the pond.

A BRIEF HISTORY OF SOUTHERN MANHOOD, continues

As nearly as I can tell, the point of hunting seems to be to deprive one's self of normal comforts and to pretend to like it. Even though his Red Wings make blisters on his heels, he refuses to buy high-tech hiking boots. Trail mix would be a dang sight easier to carry and digest. Yet for some reason he insists on heating up a can of Beanee Weenees on the hood of his truck. When he returns from a weekend of stalking and killing in the woods, the Southern hunter bellyaches about how far he had to walk, how cold it

MAN-TO-MAN SWEET TALK

Ace
Slick
Bubba
Hot Shot
Hoss
Big Man
Chief
Buddy
Boss
Slim
Junior
Booger

was, how many bugs crawled into his sleeping bag. But while he ticks off this list of miseries, he's smiling from ear to ear. If he ran into those same conditions vacationing in Vegas, he'd ask to see the manager and demand his money back. But if chiggers don't bite him on a hunting trip, he feels cheated.

And then there's that bonding thing. Killing furry animals must bring men closer together in some way. The terms of endearment that a guy uses for his hunting buddies prove it. Ace, Chief, Slick, Hoss—those sweet nothings sound almost as affectionate as Honey Pie, Sweetie, Sugar, and other love names a man reserves for the woman in his life. A fellow's most adored hunting companion doesn't fall for hokey pet names, however; he responds to a whistle and loves his master unconditionally.

The feeling is mutual. The Southern outdoorsman wonders: What's *not* to love about a dog? A dog never shoots first, never disagrees on moral grounds. He's without obnoxious opinions about politics or sports. A loyal hound lets a fellow go anywhere he wants, never expects a phone call or a commitment, and he has yet to pout, or complain, or badger a man to talk more about his feelings. The Southern hunter hopes he'll never have to choose between his bird dog and his wife. After all, he can always stick something frozen in the microwave, but he'll never find a woman who'll hold a point or retrieve quail.

A man in Texas paid a lawyer a $10,000 retainer plus $300 per

1925   The Grand Ole Opry goes on the air in Nashville. Alabama's Crimson Tide wins the national football title.

hour to help him win custody of his dog in an ugly divorce. It's not unusual to hear a Southerner describe his dog as a valet, a gentleman's gentleman, Jeeves in a hair suit. "He brings my slippers, wakes me up in the morning. If only I could teach him to drive."

The Southern man prefers a functional dog—a bird dog, coon dog, guard dog. And the Dixie woodsman's canine companion must be a mongrel. No pedigreed "Gucci poochies" are allowed in the woods when a band of liquor-loosened weekend warriors whoops it up. He won't have a yappy little lapdog either. "Those are for women." A proper man's dog should be big, lazy, and often smelly—sometimes, in fact, a mirror reflection of the Good Old Boy himself. And the Southern woman has learned that a good dog—like a quality Southern man—can double as a comforter, a dishwasher, a home security system, and a conversationalist.

That's right, conversationalist. Many Southern men swear their dogs can talk. My grandfather's dog Droopy used to stand beside his chair at mealtime and demand, "I want roast." Another fellow insisted that his pooch spoke to his wife during dinner by growling "I'm hungry, little Alma." The crazy thing about it, the dog owner said, was that they never could quite place the accent.

Some Southern papas have felt moved to name a child after a particularly beloved hunting dog. "Dobie Marie" makes a nice name for the daughter of a man with a prized Doberman called guess what. Or how about "Stonewall Shepherd" for a boy? A gentleman friend from Mississippi adopted two strays not long ago and couldn't settle on names. When a business trip took him to New York for a few days, he carried along a snapshot of the pups in hopes that inspiration might strike in transit. He showed the photo to a waiter at 21 and asked his opinion.

How about "Crazy" for the lively one and "Lazy" for the more lackadaisical? No, the Mississippian decided, a dog's name is too important to be a joke. Eventually he christened one of the mutts after his ex-wife and the other after his girlfriend. From his point of view, he had paid both women an enormous tribute.

A man without a good dog

DIXIE BOY TV

The Andy Griffith Show
The Beverly Hillbillies
Green Acres
Petticoat Junction
The Dukes of Hazzard
Carter Country
Matlock
Evening Shade
In the Heat of the Night

"THAT'S MR. MONGREL TO YOU!"
Dog Insult Linked to Slaying
—headline from *The Jackson Clarion-Ledger.*

probably fishes more than he hunts. There's less preparation involved. A line, a pole, a crawdad hole, and bingo! he's in business. Give a man a few minutes to pick up a carton of worms and a six-pack at the convenience store and he's practically frying bream already. Unless, of course, he's a fly fisherman. With those guys, months of cornball philosophizing and trying on waders at Orvis have got to precede catching a measly trout pretty enough to kiss and small enough to throw into an aquarium. Your average Dixie boy doesn't have the patience for tying feathers and beads to a fishing hook.

The Southerner might call in sick to work when the fish are biting, but he won't take part in just any wilderness romp. Hiking really isn't his style. Neither is bird-watching, unless he's holding a gun watching for a covey of quail to fly up out of the brush. You won't likely find a Southern man riding a mountain bike, or snow boarding at Vail until temperatures begin to drop to Hell. And since *Deliverance*, the Dixie boy has said a big "no thanks" to white-water rafting.

When it comes to movies, the Southern man craves action, John Wayne, big breasts, and flicks where the Communists get what's coming to them. Clint Eastwood was okay until he started cluttering up his westerns with moral messages. That Ernest guy tickles the Dixie boy's funny bone. And though he wouldn't say so to his wife, he thought *Thelma and Louise* was more than a little scary. Sometimes he whispers "I'll be back" or "Hasta la vista, baby" to his reflection while he's shaving. And though he's no pervert, he wouldn't mind going skinny-dipping with the Little Mermaid. "You know, if she wasn't a cartoon and all."

The Good Old Boy believes prime-time television has been sliding slowly down the toilet since they canceled *Gunsmoke*. He thinks Homer Simpson is kind of funny, and Roseanne would be hilarious if she wasn't a girl. Sometimes the macho Southern viewer can't help yelling at the set and advising Roseanne to clean up her act and drop a few pounds. He starts telling Matlock who done it before the second set of commercials. And it ticked off the whole family whenever he'd warn Joe Mannix where the bad guys were hiding. "Joe! Watch out for that goofy sumbitch with the switchblade!"

The Southern Gentleman never screams at the screen. He insists that he doesn't watch much television at all except an occasional Masterpiece Theatre episode. Yet he mysteriously knows "Turbo" from "Ice," lets slip that he thought Mary Tyler Moore mistreated Dick Van Dyke, admiringly mentions Aunt Bea Taylor's full figure and good cooking, and confesses that he knew all along there was something going on between Greg Brady and his TV mom.

When he's blue, if there's not a game on TV and it's too late in the season to read girlie magazines in the deer stand, the Dixie boy occasionally stoops to entertain himself with other hairy-chested diversions. Anything involving the use of dangerous power tools keeps him busy on Sunday between the end of church and Fred Couples' televised tee-off.

The Southern handyman's tips for a perfect fix-it job? Take the washing machine apart. Get frustrated. Lose all interest in fixing it. Leave the parts scattered in the driveway for at least a week, until somebody calls a professional. Finally—and this is the most important part—when the repairman arrives, hound him by telling him the proper way to do the job.

But a fellow can't always rely on the washing machine going out when he's hungry for excitement. While Atlanta or Nashville offers the big-city sophistication of driving ranges and all-night video arcades, good times in small towns involve honky-tonking, raising hell, and

visiting. In some wide spots in the road a can of beer and a bug zapper is a hot Saturday night. When the volunteer fire department stages a jaws-of-life demonstration, the Good Old Boy brings a date.

In his never-ending quest to push the outer edge of the relaxation envelope, the adventurous Southern man seeks a diversion that combines as many of his favorite things as possible. For example, if they ever played a football game with fast cars zipping around the cinder track and used good dogs to retrieve downed linemen—ah! it'd be Redneck nirvana.

Thanks to that crazy Charlotte banker in his Alka-Seltzer suit, a little slice of lollygagging Heaven slipped from the South's grasp. See, Charlotte's competition in the bid to score an NFL franchise was Memphis. The Memphis team, to be owned partially by Elvis Presley Enterprises, was to have been known as the Hound Dogs. Who knows? Dale Earnhardt and Bill Elliott might have been persuaded to drive a halftime show. Sitting there in the La-Z-Boy watching the Hound Dogs whip the tar out of the—oh, if only the Yankees were a football team. A fellow can dream, can't he?

CHAPTER SIX

Mama

Queen of His Heart

IN SMALL TOWNS RUMORS GET AROUND FASTER than a coon dog picks up fresh tracks. For years a dishy piece of dirt has floated around our town about this particular widow's devotion to her only son.

The first part of the buzz involves the special way the old gal taught Sonny the facts of life. Supposedly one day when the boy was about seventeen, Mama hollered him into the house. "Son, have you ever seen a grown woman naked?"

"No, ma'am," the big old hulking thing shouted back.

"Well, come here a minute then." Mama beckoned him into the bathroom where she was soaking in the tub. When he walked in, she stood up. "Now you have. Run on back out and play."

The second part of this gossip just gets me every time. Seems this six-foot son of hers was a high-school and later college football star. Some mornings after especially heartbreaking gridiron defeats, local folks swear they would see the letterman's mama sitting on her front porch rocking him in her lap. "Bless his heart," she would say, "he's upset about that bad old fumble."

Even in a region like this one where motherhood and sainthood stack up as pretty much one and the same, people in our town concluded, *"That* really is too much."

When Southern men talk about "mother's love and sacrifice," they mean "for Mother's love, I'll sacrifice." In both black and white Dixieland households, Mama runs the show. The South functions as a matriarchy in full flower. Today's grown-up Southern man might earn his keep down at the office with Daddy, and he might whoop and holler in the woods with the other boys, but no matter how far he roams or how often he marries, the sure-enough Dixie boy's most natural habitat is at home with Mama, queen of his heart.

This mama-worship thing should come as no news flash to those familiar with the peculiar ways of Beulahland. As a male creature in such a lush, feminine environment, the Southern man stands in slack-jawed awe of woman's power to give life. He never takes Mother's love for

THE FRONT PORCH:
Blue Hairs

THINK OF THEM as steel magnolias, widow women with aqua-rinsed hairdos. Geriatric belles to be reckoned with, Blue Hairs represent the true backbone of a rigid region.

Southern Blue Hairs come in a variety three-pack. Writer Florence King has categorized them as "Dear Old Things," "Rocks," and "Dowagers." She separates them by weight, like prizefighters. The Dear Old Thing is a little old lady, a featherweight. The Rock is a big old lady, a bantamweight. A Dowager is a huge old lady, a heavyweight Dixie-bred Blue Hair. All three types dodder around most every Southern town, big or small, wearing orthopedic shoes and clutching silver-topped walking canes. You'll find them at the Garden Club, the bridge table, or poring over genealogy records for the DAR. Blue Hairs flirt with young men and menace young women. Bosoms heaving, they keep the gossip mill churning and generally make things tick.

In a region where dainty beauty is everything, a past-her-prime Blue Hair relies on something else—power. She pretends to be scatterbrained while cataloguing several generations' worth of information in a steel-trap mind. She wins the affections of everything in pants by speaking up against feminism. Then she proceeds to run the town.

"I never worked a day in my life. I know a woman's place," she'll say to some admiring young Southern Gentleman. "Now, pour me another touch of that sherry, boy. I've decided that we're going to run you for Congress."

A BRIEF HISTORY OF SOUTHERN MANHOOD, *continues*

granted. He just can't thank the old girl enough for getting him here all safe and sound.

At a ceremony celebrating the state of Georgia's centennial way back in the 1830s, a gallant gentleman issued this toast: "Woman! The center and circumference, diameter and periphery, sine, tangent and secant of all our affections!" Well, I'm here to tell you "woman" was a euphemism; what the toastmaster really meant was "Mother!"

From the Virginia Tidewater, to the hollers of Tennessee, to the bayous of Louisiana, and practically everywhere in between, the only thing most men hold more dear than watching football and bass fishing is You Know Who. A widow in Dixie never need worry about who will care for her in old age as long as she's got a son. That's a boon for Southern women all around. Caring sons make good husbands, and a man who values his mother will value his children. No matter how you look at it, this Mama hangup shakes out as a positive aspect to the Southern man's personality. Unless it gets out of hand.

In Mississippi, a sixty-year-old Southern Gentleman with adult children and grandchildren of his own lost his mama a few years ago and now considers himself an orphan. Texas pianist Van Cliburn called his mother "Little Precious." Former pro-football great Earl Campbell mentioned his mom at nearly every postgame press conference. Elvis dyed his hair jet black so it'd match his mother Gladys' ebony locks. Remember Miss Lillian, Jimmy Carter's mother? Some called Virginia Kelley, Bill Clinton's mom, "the Miss Lillian of the 1990s."

But just because a man has a mother doesn't necessarily mean he's a Mama's Boy; although if he's a Southern man, it would not be a foolish bet. A Southern girl who needs to know if she's hooking up with just an average doting son or a hopelessly devoted Mama's Boy should ask herself these questions: Did she outfit him in darling little Lord Fauntleroy suits right up until he started shav-

101 USES FOR KUDZU
#97—Free souvenir of your vacation in Dixie.

A BRIEF HISTORY OF SOUTHERN MANHOOD, continues

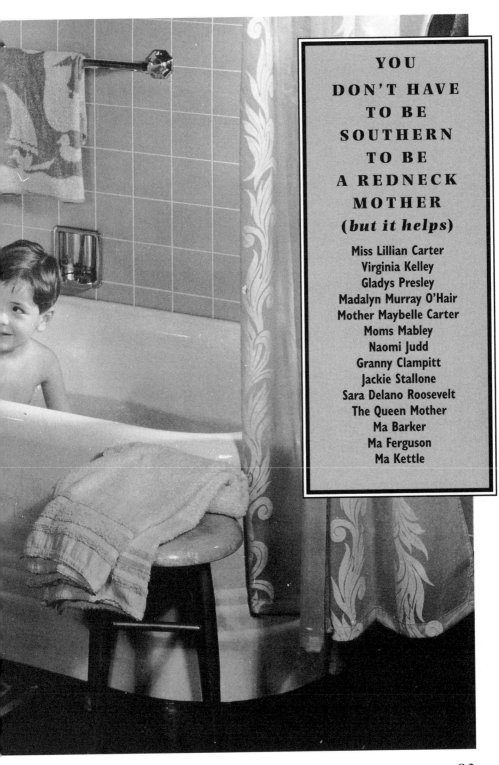

YOU DON'T HAVE TO BE SOUTHERN TO BE A REDNECK MOTHER (*but it helps*)

Miss Lillian Carter
Virginia Kelley
Gladys Presley
Madalyn Murray O'Hair
Mother Maybelle Carter
Moms Mabley
Naomi Judd
Granny Clampitt
Jackie Stallone
Sara Delano Roosevelt
The Queen Mother
Ma Barker
Ma Ferguson
Ma Kettle

1936   *Gone With the Wind* is published.

ing? Did she prohibit his father from taking him to the barbershop, instead letting his hair grow long and curling it herself? Did she iron a load of T-shirts and boxer shorts each week, and then mail them to him at college?

Does he buy her expensive jewelry? Drive her to bridge club? Does he drop a girlfriend when Mama sniffs, "She's common"? Does he even *have* girlfriends? And here's the big one: Does he know the name of his mother's silver pattern? If he throws around words like "Gorham" or "Reed and Barton"—honey, you've got a deep-voiced, bewhiskered baby on your hands.

Around here, a touch of the Mama's Boy is really a normal part of a healthy male personality. Most Southern men treat their mamas like queens. Grown men across the region felt as if country singer Jimmie Rogers were speaking for them personally whenever he performed "Mother, Queen of My Heart." The mother-loving Southern boy battling a guilty conscience probably identifies with Merle Haggard's rendition of "Mama Tried" or Johnny Paycheck lamenting "I'm the Only Hell (My Mama Ever Raised)." Hank Williams' Nashville-style dirge "Message to My Mother" deals with the unspeakable—Mama's death. Some lachrymose Southern men can hardly listen to that one at all. Southern Gentlemen and Good Old Boys agree: "Mama, well, she was about half saint is all."

"How's your mama and them?" is a common Southern salutation.

HOW TO CHARM HIS MAMA

Take his last name without a hyphen.
Comment on her silver.
Ask her how to fix sweet potato pie just the way he likes it.
Agree with her opinions about the trashy neighbors.
Don't let him lose weight.
Name your first daughter after her.
Don't be flashy.
Join the DAR or the Junior League.
Let her beat you in bridge.
Get a divorce and give him back to her.

A BRIEF HISTORY OF SOUTHERN MANHOOD, continues

A good answer would be "Overbearing, thank you very much." A Yankee I know told me about an unnerving encounter he had with an unabashed Southern mama's boy. After a business dinner, my Northern friend stopped by his Southern colleague's house for a nightcap. In the burly paneled den, as the two men sipped bourbon, the host asked my friend, "You want to see something adorable?"

The Yank nodded, assuming he was about to meet some prized bird dog's new pup. His host hurried from the room and returned carrying a framed photograph. "This"—he beamed, revealing a portrait of a 1930s debutante—"is my mother. Did you ever in your life see anything so precious?"

Lucky for my friend, he coughed up the right answer. Tell a Southern man that he has no future, call him ugly, steal his car. But don't ever, for any reason, make a disparaging comment about his relatives, especially his mama, unless you just feel like seeing your intestines spilled on the sidewalk. I wouldn't advise combining the words "yo' mama" even with the best intentions below the Mason-Dixon. If you accidentally let it slip—*"You talking about my mama? Huh? You talking about my mother?"*—that's what you'll hear right before your world goes black. Before calling a Southern man a "son of a bitch," it'd be smart to have your will drawn up.

In Texas, a county commisioner once slathered some harsh words on a county judge. The judge retaliated by calling the commish "a sorry bastard." Following a big hoo-ha in the local papers, the judge took it back, sort of: "I apologize to your mother. She is a very nice lady." For the commissioner that was the cruelest blow of all. His mama had been dead for about eight years.

A true Mama's Boy never outgrows his affection. His first love remains the greatest love of his life. "Y'all ever watch *Jeopardy?*" a middle-aged Good Old Boy asked his buddies one night.

The fellows shook their heads, no.

"It's fun. I play with Mama and Daddy nearly every afternoon. They can't get any answers. I beat the hell out 'em."

"Mama" is nearly eighty years old. "Daddy" just turned ninety-three. And this never-married Southern boy still lives at home and sleeps in the same bedroom where he grew up. Around here, nobody finds this arrangement strange.

"You beat them every day?" One of his pals smelled a rat.

"Yep, every day."

"Hmmm," the skeptical friend said. "I'll bet your mama lets you win."

I know a woman whose mother-in-law calls every morning to ask what her son ate for breakfast. "Didn't touch his bacon? Did he look pale? Did he remember his overcoat?"

At a cocktail party, I overheard a lawyer friend tell a complete stranger: "Ask anybody—my mother was *the* most beautiful woman ever to graduate from Lee High School. Ever! I tell you, she's a cutie."

I have a girlfriend who fell in love with a thirty-something Dixie bachelor. She says he brings up Mama's virtues every chance he gets. He tells about how his mother worked her way through college, and how she learned how to fly an airplane so she could make the commute from the farm to the city and back fast enough to get supper on the table for her family every evening after work. Like most Southern belles, my pal has heard this Super Mom song before, and she knows she'll never quite measure up. On the other hand, she also knows when she has a son of her own she'll be wearing the Mama crown herself for the rest of her life.

Southern mother love seldom goes unrequited. The mother of Texas congressman Charles Wilson reportedly once telephoned Speaker Tip O'Neill demanding that her son not be sent to Central America again on congressional business. Worried that harm might come to her forty-five-

BELLE OR BEAU?

The belle pretends to swoon.
The belle suffers from egomania.
The belle fudges the facts about
her chastity.
The belle likes to dress up
in fancy gowns.
The belle pretends the beau
runs the show.

The beau pretends not to swoon.
The beau suffers from insecurity.
The beau fudges the facts about
his promiscuity.
The beau likes to dress up
in fancy uniforms.
The beau pretends the belle
runs the show.

A BRIEF HISTORY OF SOUTHERN MANHOOD, continues

year-old boy in the land of Communist insurgents, Mrs. Wilson took her concerns straight to the top.

I know a doting Dixie mom who saved the toenails her son clipped and the ashes from the last cigarette he smoked before he went off to the army. Many years later, after her boy died, the woman prohibited her grandchildren from using a certain jar of mustard in the refrigerator. "Don't touch that! It was your daddy's mustard. God, how he loved it on a cold ham sandwich."

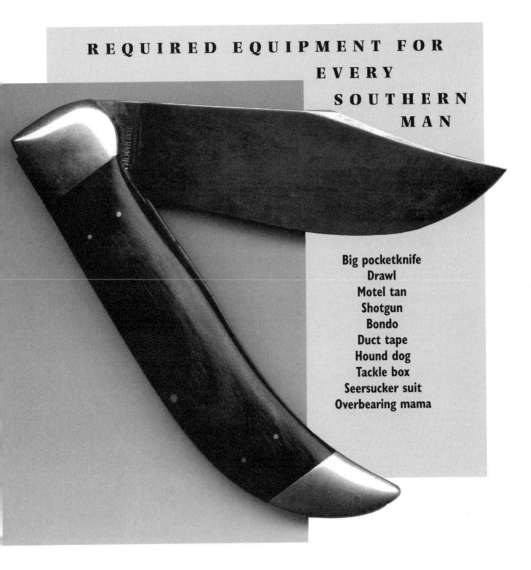

REQUIRED EQUIPMENT FOR EVERY SOUTHERN MAN

Big pocketknife
Drawl
Motel tan
Shotgun
Bondo
Duct tape
Hound dog
Tackle box
Seersucker suit
Overbearing mama

Behind every successful Southern man there's a Southern woman—not his wife, his mother. Mama teaches him everything. Which fork to use at a fancy dinner party. Not to run with scissors. Never to fry bacon in the nude. How to be a man. A New Orleans attorney says, "It all started for me at Mama's knee. Mama's way is the only way I know. She called me her 'raffle baby.' I always thought she meant she'd won me as a door prize. One day I asked her why she called me that and she said, 'Well, I took a chance on a sofa.'"

President Andrew Jackson of Tennessee credited his mom with instilling in him the correct patriarchal values he needed to get to the White House. "She was as gentle as a dove and as brave as a lioness," he said. "The memory of my mother and her teachings were after all the only capital I had to start life with."

A swinging, forty-five-year-old Southern playboy told me not long ago, "Mama wants me to get married by the end of the year. Time is running out and I'm frantic. It just breaks my heart to disappoint her."

Now, just because he's a Mama's Boy doesn't necessarily mean he's a wimp or a sissy. Don't even think about using that S-word to describe him. The mere suggestion of any gray area between the sexes can cause the Southern man to go to pieces, to just break down and have himself a good cry. "Not me," he says when presented with the theory that every man has a feminine side. "I'm all man. Aren't I, Mama? "

Maybe the Dixie boy feels compelled to announce his masculinity so loudly and obnoxiously all the time because he's ashamed of being caught sitting in his mama's lap. So when he's not being coddled, he shoots rifles into the air, skins rabbits with his bare hands, and jacks his truck up on big balloon tires to assert his manliness. Sometimes desperation pushes him to extremes. That's when the especially crude Good Old Boy gets drunk, drops his trousers, and hollers, "Hey, y'all. Looky here at Mr. Wiggles."

Dixie boys pick up this insecurity paranoia from their dads. As much as the Southern man loves and adores his mama, he admires and fears his daddy. For the Southern son, it's always Mama and Daddy, not Mother and Father, or Mom and Dad, and never Daddy *then* Mama. Mama comes first. Daddy might make the money, but Mama pays the bills. Mama doles out food and affection and punishment, while Daddy

A BRIEF HISTORY OF SOUTHERN MANHOOD, continues

holds high expectations. The Southern pop might be king of his own castle, but the Southern mom is prime minister. And as all good royalists will remember, the monarch is just a figurehead; the PM runs the show.

While Mama inculcates domestic and moral values, Daddy delivers assertiveness training. When Daddy implores that his son quit whining, buck up, and be a man, Mama comforts the little fellow, drying his tears, burying his head in her bosom, and telling him what a good boy he is. The weirdest part of the whole family drama is that Daddy probably got comforted by his mama in this way, and his daddy and his daddy's daddy too. And this is the way the Southern son will raise his own children. He'll honor his daughter, treat her like a princess; and he'll be stern with his son, who will then run to *his* mama for comfort.

Fine sons grow into dandy dads. One gentlemanly Southern father, a millionaire widower, thought nothing of taking time out from his busy work day to call each of his daughter's nine bridesmaids just to figure out who picked up the wrong pair of wedding shoes. That same loaded Pop had his picture printed on play money for his daughter's debutante ball. The party's theme was "Daddy's Money," and below the patron's likeness on each bill was the slogan IN DADDY WE TRUST. When the band took a break, the deb's papa took the stage and belted out "My Girl."

Sometimes, even a mother's kindest son does bad. I read about a socially prominent Mama's Boy in Savannah who ran into a spot of trouble with the law. Accused of killing the man who lived with him, this good son went to jail. While he awaited trial, the accused murderer reportedly planned a fancy party for his mother. From his jail cell, he masterminded the whole affair, phoning repeatedly to make sure the fountain was turned on and that the flowers arrived on time.

Not even steel bars can separate a boy and his mama. Or a mama from her boy. In my hometown when a young man stood trial for murder, his mother sat in the courtroom dressed in an outfit identical to his—blue jeans and a flannel shirt—as a show of solidarity. Mother-son dressing: You won't see that anywhere but Dixie.

Sometimes the guys you least expect turn out to be the biggest Mama's Boys of all time. I remember a hard-drinking, foul-mouthed, overweight store proprietor in our town. Rumor was that he sold pornography and ran illegal card games in the back of his shop. But everybody

1942 Texan Jo-Carrol Dennison becomes the first Southerner crowned Miss America.

89

liked him. He was jolly and kind, and he didn't mind letting good customers take a candy bar on credit.

Anyway, this bachelor businessman shared a house with his elderly mother. (The word on her was that she made a fortune as a prostitute during the 1920s but had fallen on hard times since losing her looks.) One afternoon I ran into the store to get a Coke and caught the proprietor just before he closed. "Why are you closing so early?" I asked.

"Oh, me and Mama are going out to supper. I have to get home early to help her put on her makeup and squeeze her into her panty hose."

If you could only have seen this man's mama, you'd know all there was to know about love and devotion.

CHAPTER SEVEN

Old Times Here Are Not Forgotten

Pruning the Family Tree

❝THE PRINCE OF WALES WAS BORN IN RICHmond," Will Rogers once said. "Richmond, England, not Richmond, Virginia. He didn't have enough ancestors to be born a Virginian."

If you've ever spent any time in America's Richmond—or Natchez or Charleston or Savannah, for that matter—you know that Will Rogers roped himself a truism with that one. Down South folks cultivate more than cotton. We also prune family trees. It's that strong sense of family history that gives the Southerner roots. Those roots, and probably a mortgage, bind him to Dixieland.

All Southern history is really family history. The Southerner loves his kinfolk, and not just those with hearts still beating. Where the Westerner crows loudly about his own accomplishments, the Southern boy brags through the back door.

Family binds the Southern Gentleman to Dixie, and loyalty to the land holds the Good Old Boy. While the Gentleman pays homage to his ancestors, the Good Old Boy sings the praises of his homestead. For both types, home can be a pretty convoluted concept. It's a region, a house, a town, or simply where Mama lives or is buried. Whether his birth country bears cotton, lumber, tobacco, or the oozing mud of the Mississippi, today's Southern boy gets all misty just thinking about the spot where he and his mama were once one.

Many Southerners agree with William Faulkner, who felt that his homeland got downright lucky when natural gifts were being handed out: lucky in that God did so much for the region and man has done so little. There are those who'll tell you that savoring the beauty of the South requires an appreciation for the grace and dignity of wild things left undisturbed—including Southern men.

It's no big surprise that Southerners get so attached to home and family and the land. While the arid scrub of the West encourages movement, the damp leafy canopy of the South invites nesting. Tumbleweeds hurry across the Western plains, while hardwoods hug the black-velvet dirt of Dixie. The West says, "Move along, son." But the South beckons, "Settle down, take your shoes off, stay awhile."

And you can bet that when the land talks, the Southerner listens. Black man or white, hick or aristocrat, the Dixie boy acts as midwife to the land; he respects its fertility, helps it bear. More than likely he can

THE FRONT PORCH:
White Trash

*I*T'S NOT *a compliment, and it has racist overtones. But it's still funny, sometimes, as long as the White Trash being ridiculed isn't you.*

White Trash is not a state-of-the-art slur. Travelers coined it at least a century ago when observing that white Southern society consisted of two tiers: plantation proprietors at the top and wretchedly deprived dirt farmers at the bottom. This stereotype stuck. Burt Reynolds even made the lower tier seem rather cool in the "hick flick" movies of the 1970s. But not cool in a lasting way. These days the words White Trash bring to mind images of wife-beating, racism, illiteracy, incest, and, oddly, religious fundamentalism. Go figure.

How to recognize renaissance White Trash? It's tricky. You might consider an ever-present toothpick protruding from a toothless smile to be a strong indicator. When you ask for directions to his house, and he responds, "You got good tires?"—there's a hint. A pickup truck doesn't necessarily peg a man as basura blanco. *But a four-by-four with Yosemite Sam* BACK OFF! *mud flaps might. And those mud flaps featuring a shiny silhouette of a naked, cartoon woman? Bingo! Baby, the fellow driving that vehicle is the genuine article.*

But Yankees, listen up: Southern and White Trash are not interchangeable terms. Call a fellow a clay-eater, a Redneck, a cracker, a yokel, a hillbilly, a sharecropper, but best not to call him White Trash. As I said before, it's not a compliment.

A BRIEF HISTORY OF SOUTHERN MANHOOD, continues

identify every bush, tree, and flower near his home. And even if he's not a farmer, he always seems to know the best times to plant. The Southern man lives *in*, not *on*, his environment.

He probably calls each mutt in town by name. He remembers the perfume of the first girl he kissed, and when the radio plays a particularly sad country song, he mumbles, "Damn it," and tries not to draw attention to himself as he wipes a tear from his eye. When a Southerner strolls through a cemetery—as he'll often do—each headstone brings to mind a story about an ancestor, a neighbor, or a neighbor's ancestor.

Once he gets warmed up, he routinely imbues forebears with stupendous powers:

"Miss Mama Lady, my grandmother on my daddy's side, split logs, butchered hogs, was a fine shot and oh! such a lovely dancer. Little, itty-bitty woman, hated Commies even worse than Yankees. Why, she walked right up to this fellow Jimmy Jack Crucheff from over at Mobile one morning and slapped him as big as you please before she realized he was no relation to Mr. Nikita Khrushchev, the Red. Always a lady, she later baked Jack a peach cobbler. Turns out he hated pinkos nearly as much as she did. They were fast friends right up until the day Miss Mama Lady laid down and died at the John Birch Society Christmas Dance in 1965. Oh! She was sure something. Have I ever told you about—"

It's not a new phenomenon. Pioneering Southern colonists started this ancestor worship soon after setting up camp in America and harvesting fortunes in cotton and tobacco. Once they got the plantations running smoothly, they had time to embellish their pasts. By cracky, if some peckerwood suddenly found himself as rich as a king, shouldn't he have some royal relatives back there somewhere?

Buying an obscure title from cash-strapped Euro-trash royalty has been from time to time an American vogue, but innovative Southern social climbers found an easier way to nobility: Just pick yourself a title and go to using it.

British is the peerage nine out of ten Southerners

101 USES FOR KUDZU
#19—Keeps old people in their homes.

A BRIEF HISTORY OF SOUTHERN MANHOOD, continues

recommend most. Such Anglophiles are Dixie boys, in fact, that they've gone and put an Oxford in eight Southern states. For the status-hungry Southerner, bearing an English title roughly equals dying and going to Heaven, but in a pinch any old dukedom will do.

A fellow in Memphis recalls that in the early 1950s the names "Lord and Lady Fields" began showing up bold-faced in local society columns. The lordship and his lady had not immigrated from the far reaches of the empire. Although they did speak with unusual accents—sort of a Birmingham, Alabama, meets Birmingham, England, patois. Not long after a much-ballyhooed painting of then Princess Elizabeth of Great Britain gussied up in the Order of the Garter appeared on the cover of *Life* magazine, engraved invitations arrived at fine addresses throughout the Memphis area. "Please join Lord and Lady Fields for the official unveiling of a portrait of their daughter, Lady Something or Other . . ."

> # MEN
> # WITH
> # A SENSE
> # OF HERITAGE
> # DO NOT . . .
>
> . . . slash tires
> . . . spray graffiti on overpasses
> . . . walk on graves
> . . . worry about tomorrow
> . . . dodge the draft
> . . . forget to vote
> . . . insult women
> . . . wear hats indoors
> . . . forgive
> . . . forget

Well, when guests entered Fields' Manor on the evening of the grand soiree, they were confronted by a large oil painting of a standard-issue Southern belle dressed entirely in the Order of the Garter and looking uncannily like the soon-to-be Queen of the British Empire. On a hall table situated directly beneath the great work, a copy of a certain issue of *Life* was casually but conspicuously displayed for the benefit of those too obtuse to make the connection between European and Tennessee royalty.

Even without such step-saving shortcuts to the peerage as Lord and Lady Fields took, this ongoing good-family quest can get out of hand. Right this very minute there's probably a Southern Gentleman elbow-deep in birth records at a courthouse somewhere, desperate to squeeze a drop of regal sap from his family tree. What he finds he'll milk for all it's worth. What he can't find,

1946 B. B. King thumbs a ride to Memphis and starts playing the blues.

he'll simply make up, and that fiction will be ten times more glorious than any truth.

Go South looking for good catfish, red-hot blues, or moonlight 'n' magnolia romance, but do not head this way looking for the straight scoop on anything. The Southern Gentleman seems genetically incapable of uttering the words "I don't know," and he's socialized against ever issuing a short answer. When he says "to make a long story short" it's usually already too late.

The gifted Southern storyteller is drawn to embellishment like the Devil's drawn to bad. Ask him what time it is, and he'll tell you how to make a clock. Let slip anything about the Civil War, and you may as well order another cup of coffee because he's about to ramble into a numbing litany about the lengths to which great-great-aunt Sister went to keep Sherman's grimy Yankee mitts off the family silver. And he won't stop with where she buried the sugar bowl. Oh, no. He has to draw a picture of the particular pattern she stashed, describe what sort of shovel she used, and give exact measurements on the hole she dug.

Welcome to the Southern past-perfect world. What's past is perfect to a Southern man. He perfects it himself, adding a flourish here and there, custom tailoring the events of a century ago to fit his own present-day dimensions. He then goes on to retell these little hand-painted reminiscences so often, and so well, that the fiction slowly becomes memory.

As far as the big picture goes, textbooks keep him honest. He finds, and masterfully mines, some latitude in the close-ups. He can't very well maintain that the Rebels whipped the Yanks at Vicksburg; plenty of documentation contradicts him there. He can, however, recount in lavish language how Daddy's great-uncle Clyde Otis fought forty Yankees off the front porch using nothing but a fencing foil. While never flat-out rewriting history, the Southern storyteller cuts and pastes like crazy.

Rivaling his flair for embellishment is his penchant for creative revenge. Not actually seeking revenge, mind you, but plotting it. This applies to the

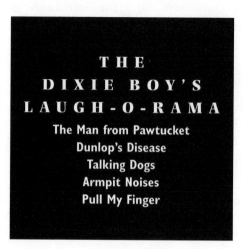

THE DIXIE BOY'S LAUGH-O-RAMA

The Man from Pawtucket
Dunlop's Disease
Talking Dogs
Armpit Noises
Pull My Finger

A BRIEF HISTORY OF SOUTHERN MANHOOD, continues

Southern Gentleman and the Good Old Boy alike. A Dixie boy might not be able to hang on to money for long, but he can sure hold a grudge until it's time to spit in the fire and call the dogs.

There's a story floating around Atlanta about a local boy who went east to school and fell in love with a Yankee girl. One evening shortly after becoming engaged, he dined with the girl's grandparents at their home.

BUMPER STICKER

U.S. OUT OF NORTH CAROLINA.

During the meal, he commented on the flatware. "This silver looks a whole lot like the few pieces saved from my great-great-grandmother's wedding pattern."

"How odd," his hostess replied. "The man at Sotheby's who appraised it for us insisted that it is handmade and one of a kind. It's been in our family since—I guess ever since the Civil War."

Well, that Southern boy stood up right then and there. "Ma'am, this silver is stolen!" He threw down his napkin and stormed out of the house. Shortly thereafter the ill-fated engagement was called off. The boy's family sighed with relief. Such "mixed marriages," they'd believed all along, are never really a good idea.

Sometimes it seems as if the Southern male licks his wounds so continuously that they never have a chance to heal. The Good Old Boy will pick at a psychological scab until it festers and ruptures. He'll be bitter about a football loss, a stolen girlfriend, or a dispute over property lines not only for a lifetime, but he'll hand those hard feelings down to his son. Sometimes rancor between families simmers for generations in the hills of Appalachia. That legendary unpleasantness between the Hatfields and the McCoys, for instance, made the Capulets and Montagues seem almost neighborly.

Could be that feuds among hill folk unfold with such unusual passion because the families involved might be a little, well, a little "closer" than most. People joke about Jerry Lee Lewis, but cousins marrying makes sense to the Southerner. If you link up with a cousin, he maintains, you can be sure she's from a good family—your own.

While the Southern Gentleman identifies strongly with authentic or slightly fudged royal antecedents, the Good Old Boy longs to feel kingly too. That scoundrel is contentment personified when sitting upon a throne. Be it a cane-bottomed rocking chair on the crumbling front porch of a shotgun shack, or a leather-upholstered chairman's seat at the end of a long boardroom table, the Southern male goes glassy-eyed when imagining that he's master of all he surveys.

Ever pass a country store and notice a pair of old boys chewing the fat out front? They are not just killing time; those guys are admiring their realm. No matter how dinky the empire, the Southerner adores it because it's his. As he looks out over the chickens scratching in his yard, he's likely to launch a stream of tobacco juice into the dust and exclaim with a self-satisfied grin, "It just don't git much better 'n this."

A BRIEF HISTORY OF SOUTHERN MANHOOD, continues

1950   First superspeedway for stock-car racing opens in Darlington, South Carolina.

A sharp-eyed belle can size up a fellow's empire right fast. If you've spent much time in Dixie, you too can probably estimate a man's net worth and social standing simply by noticing the quality of the scrap iron in his yard. Let me explain.

A Southern guy I met opened the door to his antebellum wearing house slippers, baggy khakis, and a raggedy Clemson T-shirt. A cigarette dangled from his lips, its long ash defying gravity. Yet his house graces the list of National Historic Places, and the acreage attached has yielded thousands of bales of cotton annually for the past hundred years. He has a no-fooling Chinese Chippendale sofa parked in the living room, Sheffield silver service for fifty polished ready to go in the dining room, and upstairs rests an ornate Louis XV bed. Even without seeing the fancy carpets or antique furnishings or Greek Revival architecture, I would have recognized this guy as patrician to the bone. How? Just a few feet from the verandah sat a 1966 Lincoln nearly covered with honeysuckle, and nearby a family of cats inhabited a vintage Mercedes without wheels. A broken-down Camaro would have sent a totally different message.

A Southern man's home reveals volumes about who he is and who his ancestors were. To a musician friend who grew up on a cotton plantation, home means the smell of the autumn harvest: "I remember getting real excited after school knowing I was going to play in a trailer full of freshly picked cotton for a few hours before suppertime."

A guy in Charleston says that for him, home is a drive around the Battery and the sound of Episcopal hymns at St. Philip's. To a Cajun oilfield worker, home means good étouffée. A boy I knew growing up in the

BEULAH BOYS AT HOME

- The Southern Gentleman inherited an oil portrait of his great-great grandfather
  . . . The Good Old Boy bought "Dogs Playing Poker" at Stuckey's on the interstate.
- The Southern Gentleman hopes to someday live in a house like Jefferson's Monticello
  . . . The Good Old Boy hopes to someday live in a house like Elvis' Graceland.
- The Southern Gentleman takes the Concorde to Europe
  . . . The Good Old Boy takes Greyhound to Epcot.
- The Southern Gentleman plants azaleas in his yard
  . . . The Good Old Boy plants plastic flamingos in his yard.
- The Southern Gentleman has a hummingbird feeder on his porch
  . . . The Good Old Boy has a washing machine on his porch.

1953   Hank Williams, Sr., dies.
1954   James Brown forms the Famous Flames.

Big Thicket of East Texas says home is "where all motionless objects mildew." Another friend insists he thinks of home whenever he hears chinaberries fall *ping!* on a tin roof. On one point, though, most Southerners agree: Home refers to that spot on earth where a fellow uttered his first Rebel yell.

Current address doesn't mean diddly-squat. It's the coordinates on the birth certificate that really count. Folks say a newcomer in Winston-Salem is anyone who wasn't born there. And the old guard considers an eighty-one-year-old man in Savannah, occupying the same house for eighty years, to be more or less itinerant, just passing through.

That's why a Southerner always includes hometown when making introductions: "Have y'all met Buford, from Baton Rouge?" A Southern man sees nothing weird in saying "I've lived in Los Angeles for thirty years, but Little Rock is my home."

Two things most Southern homes have in common—a front porch and a coat of arms. They say when a Good Old Boy's porch collapses, at least one dog dies. And when the trailer shakes, the family crest invariably falls from the wall. The Southern Gentleman's lineage logo has been fired into his china or engraved on his stationery. But in all Southern households, the family's past—real or invented—lurks all around.

I met a young man in Charleston from an old, old family. He spoke rather matter-of-factly about his hometown and his family heritage and his own identity, as if they were all rolled up into one big tangled knot. He said his family arrived in South Carolina sometime in the eighteenth century. "Let's face it, people who got here before then must have been pretty desperate characters." So venerable is his family's name that he's lost count of how many ancestors were called Thomas. "I think I'm the twelfth or something, but we quit using numbers after the third or fourth."

Dixie boys can't escape the powerful pull of history and home. Aboard the riverboat *Delta Queen* once, writer Alex Haley and a fellow Southerner who'd moved north heard a moving rendition of "Amazing Grace." "Kinda makes you want to come home, doesn't it?" Haley said to his friend. College football coaching legend Bear Bryant described the South's magnetism as being like "when you were out in the field and you heard your mama calling you to dinner." Truman Capote noticed it too. He said that all Southerners come home sooner or later, even if it's in a box.

CHAPTER EIGHT

Chicken-Fried Politics

"Some Candidates Kiss Babies, I Kiss Their Mamas"

POLITICAL SCANDAL ROCKED OUR COUNTY WHEN I was growing up, and voters couldn't have been more tickled about it.

I may have some of the details wrong, but it seems our humble little Watergate started out as a prank. Just for laughs the county treasurer tacked a photo of the county judge on the courthouse bulletin board. This particular candid shot featured His Honor frolicking with some professional cuties. The Good Old Boys at the courthouse—including the judge himself—had a fine laugh about it, until the local press seized the photo and had a field day with sensational headlines like "How Are Our Tax Dollars *Really* Being Spent?"

Turns out the photograph was snapped on a political "hunting trip"—wink, wink, nudge, nudge—that included most of the county's elected officials. Today it'd hardly register as a blip on the screen, but back then the local media saw this abuse of power as a three-alarm fire. Ambitious small-town newspapermen, already drunk with post–Watergate dreams of Pulitzer Prizes, pursued evidence that official funds had paid not only for the ammo, hunting licenses, and rooms at Motel 6, but maybe also for the buxom companionship.

Soon after it hit the fan, it started stinking. The judge, a savvy graduate of the sixth grade and longtime public servant, knew hot water when he boiled in it. He issued a statement intended as damage control.

He fully realized, he said, how bad all this looked, but there was a simple explanation: "Those girls were my nieces." Someone pointed out to His Honor how inappropriate it was for a man to bounce a big-busted "niece" on his lap in such a libidinous way. "Well, distant nieces," the good judge corrected himself. "More like third cousins or something."

The judge's wife also smelled a rat, but not the one you'd think. She didn't seem a bit bothered about the possibility that her husband had committed adultery; instead she suspected a political enemy was trying to engineer his downfall. She stood by her man: "That is my husband's head in the picture, but it is not his body."

Next thing we knew, regional and national news organizations were

THE FRONT PORCH:
The Drawl

SOMEHOW a few thousand Yankees have gotten the mistaken idea that a Southerner is easier to imitate than Jimmy Durante. A Northerner who wouldn't even attempt a British accent thinks he deserves the Oscar for his dead-on vocal rendition of a Southerner.

Well, if you ask me there's nothing any sadder than a Yankee trying to use "y'all" effectively. It's pitiful, that's what. "How are yeeeeew all?" They invariably think it's singular as well as plural. Then they stretch out that yew from Brooklyn to Biloxi, and it's just sad, humiliating for them.

It's also annoying the way Yankee writers use phonetic spellings when quoting a Southern speaker. All those printed wannas and gonnas and lemmes don't do Dixiespeak justice. To savor the beauty of a Southern accent properly, it should be heard, not read.

For an aural magnolia bouquet, try a political rally. A Southern politician had rather make a speech than a dollar. Some of the finest drawls around come oozing out of office-seekers. You've heard of some Southern girls being just too pretty? Well, in a way, that's what folks say happened to South Carolinian Fritz Hollings' presidential aspirations. His accent was just too pretty, too rhythmic and civilized for Yankees to fully understand. Bill Clinton made it to the White House without shedding his drawl. Rumor has it that Clinton's friends at Oxford teased him for being able to make "shit" a four-syllable word. Even with a drawler in the White House, some folks remain nonbelievers. A community college in Chattanooga once offered a night course titled: "Success Without the Southern Accent." Around here, there's no such thing.

A BRIEF HISTORY OF SOUTHERN MANHOOD, continues

dispatching correspondents down our way. They covered the judge's story not so much for the political-corruption angle, but for the comedy quotient. And the voters loved the whole spectacle. Taxpayers felt they were finally getting their money's worth—maybe not in government services, but in quality entertainment.

Southern courthouses might not always dispense perfect justice, but count on them to deliver good soap opera. As they say, "The South may not be the nation's number-one political problem, but politics is the South's number-one problem." Or number-one solution, depending on whether you happen to be a voter or a candidate. Women boning up on Southern men should know a thing or two about politics.

The Dixie boy and politics cozy up like an old married couple, a kiss and hug, a floor and rug, perfect bedfellows. Political superstars carry nicknames like sports figures around here. People called Texas governor and sometime country-western musician W. Lee O' Daniel "Pass the Biscuits Pappy," because he first gained fame as a flour salesman using that slogan on the radio. South Carolina's Senator "Pitchfork" Ben Tillman once initiated a fistfight on the floor of the U.S. Senate. In Alabama, Governor James Folsom, Sr.'s habit of puckering up to thank his more comely female constituents for their support earned him the nickname "Kissin' Jim." Louisiana Governor Huey P. Long was "The Kingfish," and political strategist James Carville is often called "The Ragin' Cajun."

Many people credit Carville with masterminding Bill Clinton's presidential bid in 1992. In the South, kingmakers like Carville are the politicians' politicians. They work their magic in legendary smoke-filled rooms and develop powerful fan clubs. Carville has said that when he was growing up in Louisiana, many little boys dreamed of becoming politicians. And why not? The skills required for a successful career in Dixie-style public service rank among the Southern man's top aptitudes—shooting the breeze, drinking booze, and collecting some coin without any heavy lifting.

A Texas high-school

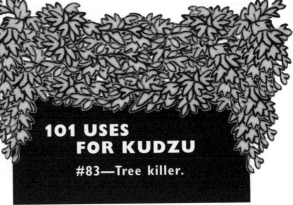

101 USES FOR KUDZU

#83—Tree killer.

A BRIEF HISTORY OF SOUTHERN MANHOOD, continues

boy recently ran for state treasurer. At age ten, Alabama's George Wallace started in politics. He tallied ballots in local elections with his father, and later said he found it as exhilarating as "watching somebody water-ski for the first time."

Remember Cooter from *The Dukes of Hazzard*? The actor who played that role told reporters how he awoke naked in a tattoo parlor in Talladega, Alabama, one night, and decided right then and there that it was time for a lifestyle change. So he ran for Congress, and won.

Every man gets the call in his own way. The Good Old Boy and the Southern Gentleman take different routes to the legislature. Think of the path of a gentlemanly lawmaker like Al Gore. He starts with a respected family name, a degree from a prestigious university, and then law school and marriage to a nice, but possibly plump, Southern debutante. It'd be great if he could save some lives on the battlefield before becoming a clerk for an important federal judge. Then a run for Congress, the Senate, and who knows what else.

The Good Old Boy's path from the trailer park to the state house can be more difficult. Bill Clinton, for example, couldn't trade on his family name, so he had to rely on his smarts. Clinton's IQ offered him a detour, but the typical road to politics for the

HEROES OF THE STUMP

Huey P. Long
Jim Folsom
James Carville
George Wallace
Theodore Bilbo
Strom Thurmond
Eugene Talmadge
Sam Erwin
Lyndon Johnson
Jefferson Davis
Edwin Edwards
Guy Hunt
Jesse Helms
Bill Clinton
Newt Gingrich
Howell Heflin
Charles Wilson

Good Old Boy likely passes the field house. A college football scholarship rescues him from the swamps or hills of his childhood. As quarterback, he joins a college frat just for the party action, and he majors in business because he's sick of being poor. Using his football fame and fraternity connections, he makes a bundle in real estate, and marries a former beauty queen. When he gets bored with making money, he runs for office.

But no matter whether he's a Good Old Boy governor or a Gentlemanly senator, the Southern politican had better be able to spin some fancy talk. Southern political rhetoric springs from the same soulful source as ragtime or jazz or gospel music. The candidate's rap gushes forth as a direct instrument of emotion. Around here the content of a political hopeful's speech matters a little, but the rhythm matters a lot. Good rhetorical rhythm reaches even the laziest ears. Listening to a gifted Southern orator deliver a spate of campaign promises is like listening to Muddy Waters wail the blues. You don't have to understand the words to know the man possesses a special gift and speaks with divine inspiration. The skilled Southern politician's message bypasses the brain altogether; it zips directly from his mouth to the voter's heart.

Somebody smart once noticed that while Italians use volume and northeastern Jews use vocabulary, Southerners get their points across with flowery adverbs and adjectives. Euphemism, rhyme, and rhythm are the tricks of the Dixie candidate's trade. And of course a well-honed regional accent doesn't hurt either. If a man on the stump can't correctly let fly contractions like "y'all," and he's not comfortable with the "fixin' to" construction, or can't drop r's when the time is right, he'll be back chasing ambulances after election day.

I've heard about certain employment want ads seeking applicants for congressional staffs in Washington, D.C., that specify "No Southern accents, please." If you ask me, that's discrimination. A Yankee congressman might not want any drawling going on in his office, but a

---

LOVE AND POLITICS

One hopelessly romantic Southern county commissioner was sentenced to ten years probation and fined $10,000 for using county funds to buy a car for a topless dancer.

A BRIEF HISTORY OF SOUTHERN MANHOOD, continues

Southern congressman won't get reelected without a magnolia accent answering his phone.

A Dixie boy's vocal lilt thickens the farther from home he wanders. That's why the most honey-dripping drawls you'll ever hear are on C-SPAN. The Deep South politician up North uses language and inflection to remind voters that he's still down-home at heart. A really well executed "y'all" on national television has become the last politically correct way to wave the Stars and Bars.

"The South might not always be right," a Southern politician exhorts, "but by God it's never wrong." That scoundrel delivers this line so well, the voter never thinks to ask "What does it mean?"

The Southern politician, at least the successful one, can say absolutely nothing so eloquently that crowds cheer and beg him to repeat it. One of Governor George Wallace's more rousing bits of oratory went like this: "Let the people be heard loud and strong. Let their thoughts be recognized in all our government says and does. The average citizen knows best what he wants and needs from a government that is truly of the people. Only when the average citizen's voice is heard do we have government responsive to the people. Never before has it been so important that the voices of the average citizens be heard and trusted as it is today."

Let me get this straight, Governor: Are you saying the average citizen should be heard? Sterling, if somewhat repetitive, vocalizing took Wallace to the Alabama governor's mansion four times—five if you count that time he got his wife, Lurleen, elected since he couldn't succeed himself. On two occasions that smooth talk took Wallace close enough to the White House for him to smell the chicken frying inside.

But George Wallace wasn't all talk. He was a fighter too, literally. Before he started running for office, he boxed. If it's not love of language that makes a Southern boy go political, it's the pursuit of a good fight. Politicians were the original Confederate warriors, remember. They took on the Yankee with rhetoric thirty years before anybody even thought about shooting at Fort Sumter. Politicians sally forth armed with the sacred spears of the South—loyalty and honor—and they use them to pick fights and win at all costs.

No matter what his party affiliation, the Southern senator or congressman or governor or county commissioner takes strong stands. He's 100 percent, unequivocally *in favor* of Family, God, Guns, and Southern

1957 Mississippi-born Craig Claiborne becomes food critic of the *New York Times*.

109

Womanhood. He stands strongly *opposed* to Sin, Evil, Greed, and New Ideas. A fellow's either for Good and Right and Honor or he's against it. If he's against it, he's a Yankee or a Communist or a carpetbagger or, worse, whatever breed of high-tech, hybrid Evil that might be. From labor organizers, to women's libbers, to health-care reformers, to foreigners selling lewd postcards, anybody who comes down here and starts trying to change things can expect a welcome about as warm as the one the boll weevils got.

I met a Good Old Boy not long ago who took time to tell me just where he and his voting friends stood on certain key issues.

On race relations: "Southerners love the individual but dislike the race. Northerners love the race but dislike the individual." Not only is this the way Southern whites feel about blacks, the white Good Old Boy said, but it's also how Southern blacks generally feel about whites. An African-American Alabaman sitting on the next barstool backed him up.

On gun control: "I'm all for a steady aim if that's what you mean."

On the New World Order: "I don't trust them Commies—still!"

Beliefs don't change much down South. It's party labels that could do with some Velcro backing. Conservative Southerners, for instance, lined up behind the Democrats' banner during Reconstruction and considered the Republicans to be wild-eyed radicals. Now it's the other way around. Dixiecrat, Populist, Democrat, Republican—no matter what his party affiliation, the Dixie boy stands for something he calls "the Southern way of life." As Mississippi's governor and later U.S. senator Theodore Bilbo once said, "Whenever the Constitution comes between me and the virtues of the women of the South, I say to hell with the Constitution." (As if anybody is ever going to come up to a Southern man on the street and say, "Okay, Buddy, which will it be: the girl or the Bill of Rights?")

Along with just about everything else around here, political drama unfolds on a romantic and very personal stage. About half the time it doesn't make much sense. Bilbo, for example, once accepted a bribe in order to gain evidence that his opponents were issuing bribes. "Kissin' Jim" Folsom championed women's rights and at the same time flaunted his reputation as a womanizer. Or consider Huey Long. At least one hundred fancy linen suits reportedly hung in his closet, yet he'd stand in front of crowds and talk down slick establishment politicians. "Those boys might have a hundred fancy suits," Long would say, "while common men like me and you are lucky to have one." Then the Kingfish would

A BRIEF HISTORY OF SOUTHERN MANHOOD, continues

1958 Jerry Lee Lewis marries his thirteen-year-old second cousin.

take off one of his expensive shoes and display the hole in his sock just to prove that he was a man of the people. And the crowd gobbled it up.

George Wallace could run on a law-and-order platform while saying this: "Of course, if I did what I'd like to do, I'd pick up something and smash one of these federal judges in the head and burn the courthouse down."

Southern demagogues—and that is not necessarily a fighting word around here—keep a few secret weapons stashed in their campaign arsenals. First thing a man needs before slinging his Panama in the ring is a little God-given charisma. Charisma is to the Southern politician what a hammer is to a carpenter. A soothing accent and good way with words come in handy around election day too. A straw hat and white linen suit couldn't hurt a man's chances, and an enemy to rail against is absolutely crucial to a hotly contested Southern campaign. When chased with violent attacks on big business, foreign aid, intellectuals, and government insiders, even the most bitter political pill will slide down easy in Dixie.

If he beats the bushes hard enough, and creatively enough, the Southern pol can find bad guys lurking all around. Theodore Bilbo once stood up against "farmer murderers, poor-folks haters, shooters of widows and orphans, international well-poisoners, charity hospital destroyers, spitters on our heroic veterans, rich enemies of our public schools, private bankers, European debt cancellers, unemployment makers, Pacifists, Communists, munitions manufacturers, and skunks who steal Gideon Bibles."

George Wallace couldn't abide by "pointy-headed intellectuals," "loose-minded, high-livin' liberals," and "briefcase-totin' bureaucreats." Jesse Helms does it with the best of them. He took a bold stand in denouncing friends of "porno kings, union bosses, and crooks."

TEMPTATION

*A*LABAMA'S GOVERNOR *Jim Folsom, Sr., reportedly once told a crowd of prospective voters: "You know what my opponents are going to do. They're going to get some good-looking blond woman, and they're going to dress her up real fine and they're going to walk her past. And friends, they're going to catch Big Jim every time."*

A BRIEF HISTORY OF SOUTHERN MANHOOD, continues

Once he's gotten himself some speeches rhythmic enough to dance to and mapped out some enemies to taunt, what else does the Dixie politician need? Well, campaign promises, of course. Every man a king. A chicken in every pot. A TV in every rec room. Pledges like those guarantee more votes below the Mason-Dixon than long dialogues about health-care reform or Eastern European foreign policy. A flamboyant personal style—you know, a carnation in the lapel or a shiny new dime for all the kiddos—also helps a guy score Xs by his name come November.

There are as many innovative ways to get votes—legal and illegal—down here as there are political candidates. A fellow running for local office in Fort Worth used to stop by all the funeral homes in town each evening and sign the bereavement books. By making points with each mourning family, he figured he picked up at least twenty new supporters for every one he lost to Heaven.

Some candidates grab voters by the stomachs at political barbecues. They say Georgia's Eugene Talmadge could draw up to 30,000 loyal followers at a single feed. Part tent revival, part picnic, these shindigs are as much a staple of Southern democracy as graveyard balloting, and they unfold according to a traditional plan.

The slop-the-electorate ritual has undergone only a few slight changes during the past hundred years. Flatbed trailers have replaced stumps as speaker's platforms. So first, the trucks roll in. Next, volunteers set up metal folding chairs from the Sunday school. Directly, teenage girls start handing out free Styrofoam hats emblazoned with the candidate's name in red, white, and blue. Kids wave miniature American and Confederate flags. Fiddlers fiddle. Everybody pigs out on pork. Grown-ups guzzle corn liquor from Dixie cups, and the host greases the electorate with oily promises of better days to come. He romances his constituents, wining and dining them, and then wining them some more. Once he gets his voter base sufficiently lubricated, he seduces them. "Just this once," he croons. "I promise. I'll still respect y'all in the morning."

At these events "Kissin' Jim" Folsom used to pass the collection bucket: "Y'all put in the suds and I'll do the scrubbing to clean up this state."

Southern politicians caught with their pants down or their hands in the cookie jar like to say "You can't make an omelet without cracking some eggs first." In Southern politics the means, no matter how ugly, always, always, always justifies the end. As Willie Stark said in *All the King's Men,* "I'll make a deal with the Devil if it'll help me carry out my programs." If only the sought-after results be deemed Good and Right, then the nastiest methods become justifiable, even glorious.

A sharp Southern pol can turn a subpoena into an asset in nothing flat. His ace in the hole? Brutal honesty. It's a gadget play for politicians in other parts of the country and a surprise in this region filled with such a long tradition of political corruption. The most beloved officeholders in Dixie raid state coffers, then stand with swelled pockets before voters and come clean. "Yes, friends, I did it. But I did it for y'all."

Whenever he's confronted with a gaffe or political blunder, one popular Southern congressman falls back on one of his most dignified excuses: "I must have been drunk."

Sinning, confessing, and sinning again isn't just a religious cycle. It doubles as a political strategy. Louisiana governor Edwin Edwards has mastered this public 'fess up and uses it to win new fans. Local lore has it that Governor Edwards once responded to questions about allegations of philandering by saying simply: "Some politicians kiss babies, I prefer kissing their moth-

THE GOOD FIGHT

*P*OLITICIANS *are the ultimate Southern warriors. In Southern politics, the end always justifies the means.*

For example, a South Carolina congressman in Washington caned a Massachusetts senator senseless in retaliation for a slanderous speech about the South. Strom Thurmond's father reportedly "had to kill a man" once because of a political feud. A few years back, Texas congressman Henry B. Gonzales slugged a fellow for calling him a Communist. And not too long ago, North Carolina's state legislature tried to pass a bill banning the sale of TV Guide *until the magazine apologized for insulting the sweet potato, a Carolina cash crop.*

A BRIEF HISTORY OF SOUTHERN MANHOOD, continues

1959 Chevrolet introduces the El Camino.

ers." On another occasion, when Edwards found himself in a politically ticklish situation, he shrugged off the trouble. "I can survive anything short of being caught with a live boy or a dead girl." He's been elected four times.

Alabama's Jim Folsom never suffered from bouts of bashfulness when he got caught doing something he shouldn't have. "Just make sure you spell my name right," he liked to say. "I'd be the first to admit I've never been a saint. I did my share of passing the goody basket around to those who supported me." God and the Southern electorate love the black sheep best. Heaven and the state house are both just a sin away.

A fed-up Southern voter carping about dishonesty in goverment once said, "Politicians are like catfish—all-mouth, no-brains, bottom feeders." Then, in the very next breath, he went on to praise his four-term incumbent representative under indictment for tax fraud, as a "scrappy sumbitch with a knack for getting things done."

Sometimes the escapades of the most endearingly human Southern politicos aren't noble, or corrupt, or statesmanlike. They're just, well, amusing. As that political scandal I mentioned earlier heated up in my hometown, our civics class took a field trip to observe the celebrity judge preside over small-claims court. His Honor entered wearing a mint-green leisure suit and white patent leather shoes, no judicial robe. Television cameras captured the action live.

Looking pleased with the media presence, the judge plunged into the crowd, shaking hands and signing autographs. He posed for a picture with some members of our class. "Mercy, mercy, look at all the pretty little girls," he said while our teacher fumbled with the focus. "I don't much like cameras. It was a camera that got me in trouble in the first place."

CHAPTER NINE

Nuts Fall Close to the Tree

A Couple of Sandwiches Shy of a Picnic

REMEMBER THE SPOOKY MOMENT WHEN YOU first realized that the charmingly insane characters of Southern folklore and fiction were quite possibly your relatives?

I must have been about twenty years old and daydreaming in the back of a Southern lit class when it happened to me. The professor was saying something about "Southern gothic" while I doodled in the margins of my spiral notebook. From a discussion of Faulkner, he launched into a monologue about dysfunctional families being fully functional in the South, normal really. And suddenly—I was knocked off my perch! Those crazy Southerners to be covered on the final exam were people *just like me!*

Yep, Faulkner, Walker Percy, Pat Conroy—all those boys wrote the gospel truth. Flannery O'Connor and Eudora Welty noticed it too. Sanity holds little charm below the Mason-Dixon where folks value "eccentrics" or "characters"—Dixiespeak euphemisms for "nut cases" or "mental patients"—as precious natural resources. As the saying goes, "Build a fence around the South and you'd have one big madhouse."

Female connoisseurs of Southern manhood can testify that eccentric boys can be as addicting as cough syrup. Why? For one thing, crazy quite often accompanies cash; the more nuts in the family tree, the more zeroes in the family fortune. Also, the nonconformist usually has a flair for fun. He tells endlessly entertaining stories, does wildly unexpected things, and is unself-consciously romantic. He might carry a mother complex, a Civil War hangup, or be haunted by the piggy man scene from *Deliverance*, but as long as his spells unfold with style, so what?

Florence King wrote, "When two Greeks meet they'll start a restaurant, two Germans will start an army, and two Englishmen will start a silence. It is not necessary for two Southerners to meet in order to start something because we have taken a little nervous problem called schizophrenia and raised it to the level of a high art."

The difference between a crazy Good Old Boy and an off-the-wall Southern Gentleman? Not much. Dixie dementia slides all around the

THE FRONT PORCH:
Humidity

WHEN YANKEES eat anything exotic in Dixie—frog legs, gator, possum—invariably they comment "It tastes like chicken." When asked about the weather down South, count on them to conclude "It's not the heat. It's the humidity."

Well, it is the humidity. The wetness hanging in the atmosphere makes every day a bad-hair day below the Mason-Dixon. It causes the cat to mildew, the car to rust, and encourages the kudzu to grow into the nursery window and strangle the baby while he sleeps. The humidity causes folks to simmer in their own gravy while waiting for the bus. It makes fat people stick to vinyl furniture. And during the heat of the summer, or the wet of the summer, the Southern humidity encourages Yankees to stay home.

Humidity leaves an imprint on the South almost as indelible as the mark left by the Civil War. A propensity for iced tea, front porches, and seersucker all grew out of the damp. The warm wetness casts the South as sensuous, feminine, fertile. Sex hangs in the Southern air, attaching itself to the water molecules. Humidity causes brow mopping, tie loosening, and skirt flapping. The moisture gives rise to naughty thoughts.

A Yankee could vacation on the planet Mercury, where the temperature reaches 800 degrees Fahrenheit in the shade if there was any shade, and he'd say, "It's not the heat. It's the humidity." A Southerner on that same trip would roll up his sleeves, pour himself a glass of iced tea, and start feeling amorous.

A BRIEF HISTORY OF SOUTHERN MANHOOD, continues

social and economic map. Rhett had a small screw loose in one area. Ashley rattled in another psychological spot. And how about Gerald O'Hara, Scarlett's dad? After the Yankees ransacked Tara, that poor fellow had a one-way ticket to berserk.

Theories about the causes of Southern insanity come a dime a dozen. Blame the weird creak in the Dixie boy's rocking chair on inbreeding, humidity, or eating dirt, and you might have yourself a subject for a master's thesis in the Southern Studies program over at Emory. No kidding, some experts sit around and think about these things full time. One of them suggested that it was a deep-seated fear of change that spurred Southerners to create such a rigidly conformist society in the first place and that insanity simply makes it possible to live in it.

The Southern outpatients themselves prefer more colorful explanations. One guy, a health researcher in the 1950s, wrote a scholarly treatise linking psychosis to air-conditioning. He put forth the idea that controlling the indoor climate might be contributing to mental illness by disturbing the balance between positive and negative ions in the atmosphere. To prove his hypothesis, the scientist needed only to point, guess where? The South.

In this most heavily air-conditioned region of the globe, you do tend to run across a fair number of outpatients walking around—sweet fellows with vacant looks, keeping cool and as happy as can be. But how then to explain all the nuts that fell from Southern trees before the window units got installed? No hands go up on that one right away, because the Southern man doesn't have a moment to spare exploring the catalyst that sent his goofy forefathers around the bend. No, siree. He's too busy holding forth about how recklessly and with what grand style they drove.

I read about a man in Savannah who glues threads to flies and takes them out for walks. The thread bobs around him as he sashays down the street. To passersby it looks as if he's flying a tiny, invisible kite. Another Georgian buzzes a crop-

101 USES FOR KUDZU

#40—Kudzu wine.

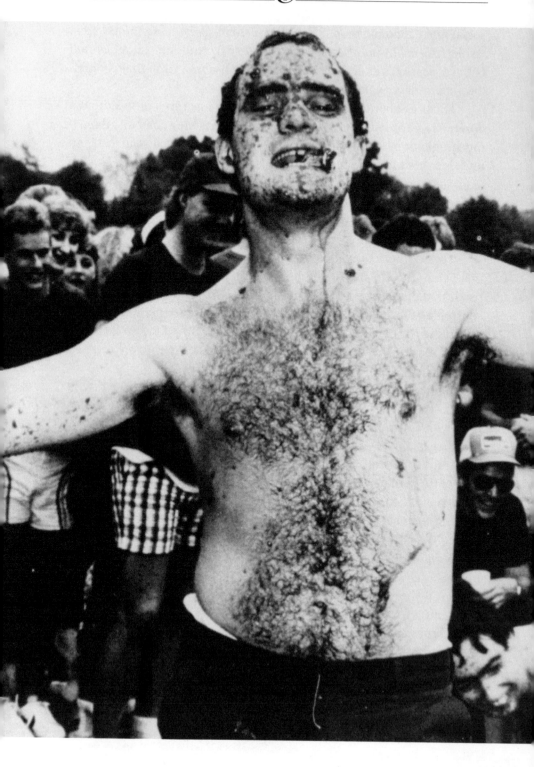

A BRIEF HISTORY OF SOUTHERN MANHOOD, continues

dusting airplane over his buddies' homes and drops bags of flour down their chimneys. In the mornings, when a Mississippi portrait artist pedals his giant tricycle across the lawn to his studio, only Yankee newcomers do a double take.

In the South, eccentricity is just about the highest form of celebrity. Being one can short of a six-pack usually constitutes a better reason to find an appreciative audience than an empty shrink's couch. Good luck trying to get a Southern man to read a self-help book. He'd rather hunt in panty hose than get in touch with his inner child. If you shake hands with a Southern fellow who's gotten years of therapy, you've just met a man with a good-looking lady doctor. Getting cured roughly equals losing your accent. When done right, mild mental illness is a gift to share grandly with those you love. "Don't hide your crazy," we say in Dixie. "Pass it around."

> **EUPHEMISMS FOR NOT QUITE RIGHT"**
>
> Not the sharpest saw in the tool shed
> A few bricks shy of a load
> The dullest knife in the drawer
> One can short of a six-pack
> A few sandwiches short of a picnic
> One fork shy of a place-setting

Why do so many goofies call Dixie home? First, guys down here live in the past; they are obsessed with days gone by. One Yankee psychiatrist managing to eke out a living down South was quoted as saying "My patients come in here and tell me so much about their crazy ancestors, I never learn what's troubling them."

Oscar Wilde noticed the same thing while traveling here more than a hundred years ago. He complained that he could scarcely admire the moon in Georgia without being told how much more spectacular it had looked before the War. Wilde attributed this hazy nostalgia to romanticism rather than dementia, but he was on to something true about the Southern psyche.

Talk about *post*–traumatic stress syndrome! The Southern man has been in denial for a least a hundred years. Somewhere in nearly every Southern male's mental makeup lurks an endearing obsession with the deeds, misdeeds, and assorted mental breakdowns of his long-dead relatives. A lunatic can hide in a Southern family like a pine needle can hide

1961 Alabama's Crimson Tide wins the national college football title.

121

in the woods. When a Southerner occupying a padded cell says, "It runs in my family," he's bragging.

Consider the peculiar way one friend boasts about her grandfather: "One Thanksgiving when I was a teenager, Grampy had this old, sorry-looking pickup truck parked in his driveway. He asked me to come out and have a look at it. He opened the hood, and I gazed right straight down to the concrete. There was no engine! Nothing! I said, 'Grampy, this truck has no motor. Why'd you buy it?'

"He just shrugged his shoulders and said, 'Just felt like I needed a set of wheels.' "

Now, that little story comes with an implied moral immediately apparent to most Southerners: "Not only am *I* kind of crazy, but I come from a long, distinguished line of fruitcakes." To call a man "lunatic" is to sweet-talk him. The Dixie-born crazy doesn't want Prozac. Hell, no! That scamp wants applause for the flamboyant spin he puts on his psychosis.

Another theory about Dixie dementia has to do with money and leisure time. Apart from acres of sterling flatware and impeccable manners, nothing screams Old South aristocracy quite like quirky behavior. Folks sitting on inherited wealth find little reason to work. That leaves them with ample time to loll around and think of new ways to act peculiar. No doubt about it: A little personality disorder forms a fine first rung for climbers of the Southern social ladder.

WE CALL HIM "COLORFUL"

Boo Radley
Ross Perot
Roger Clinton
Elvis
Bigfoot
Billy Carter
George Wallace
Little Richard
Howard Hughes
Ernest T. Bass
Forrest Gump

A BRIEF HISTORY OF SOUTHERN MANHOOD, continues

A dignified but slightly screwy gentleman in my hometown bought a brand-new Lincoln Continental every September 1. Each morning he drove it two blocks to his office, and at noon he put the car in reverse and backed home for lunch. After lunch, he returned to work in forward. At five o'clock he navigated home through the rearview mirror again, then sealed the Lincoln in the garage for the night. When September 1 rolled around next, the odometer on the year-old car read 000000 and it was time for a trade-in. That gentleman with the Lincoln didn't care a smidgen about keeping the mileage low on his land yacht. He simply wanted to remind the neighbors of his family's long-exalted social position.

Then there's chicken-fried logic. The words "Dixie" and "cognizant thought" seldom turn up in the same sentence. And for good reason. The heat at times conspires against rational problem solving, and a Southerner's penchant for passionate action sometimes makes him sloppy in his attempts at reason. The Southerner prefers sentimentality to reality. Case in point: Only a group of wild-eyed Southern eccentrics would have gone and started a war without a single cannon factory in their territory.

Just look to regional politics and religion and romance for a gumbo of skewed magnolia logic. Where but Alabama would George Wallace be hailed a statesman? Where but Louisiana would Jimmy Swaggart be canonized as a man of God?

There's a fraternity ritual at the University of Alabama where four acolytes wearing robes proceed into a darkened room carrying a huge block of ice. They place the ice on a table or makeshift altar, and the leader of the group lifts a glass of water and leads the other brothers in a toast: "To woman, lovely woman of the Southland, as pure and chaste as this sparkling water, as cold as this gleaming ice, we lift up this cup, and

BUMPER STICKER

DO UNTO OTHERS BEFORE THEY DO UNTO YOU

we pledge our hearts and our lives to the protection of her virtue and chastity."

Frat boys protecting feminine chastity? Only a Southern man could rationalize guarding the very creature he hopes to conquer.

Along with this cockeyed logic goes a penchant for refining the truth. Southerners are trained to believe what they want to believe. It's a special way of seeing the world, and it has an up side. The Southerner seldom lies. He seldom finds reason for it since he possesses such a wonderful ability to make a falsehood true in his mind before uttering it. Mastering this sort of rationalization can be trickier than teaching a pig to fly. The techniques have been honed and polished for generations, and accomplished masters of the form are venerated as Dixieland's great thinkers.

This propensity to decorate the facts helps form a cleft in the Southern psyche that allows a fellow to be puritan and hedonist at the same time, a teetotaling drunk or holy-man whoremonger.

THE WORLD CAPITAL OF WORLD CAPITALS

Root Beer Capital of the World—Gulfport, Mississippi
Watermelon Capital(s) of the World—Weatherford, Texas, and Hope, Arkansas
Fruitcake Capital of the World—Clayton, Georgia
Spinach Capital of the World—Crystal City, Texas
Frog Capital of the World—Rayne, Louisiana
Rose Capital of the World—Tyler, Texas
Strawberry Capital of the World—Plant City, Florida
Crawfish Capital of the World—Breaux Bridge, Louisiana
Speckled Perch Capital of the World—Okeechobee, Florida
Bourbon Capital of the World—Lynchburg, Tennessee
Catfish Capital of the World—Greensboro, Alabama
Collard Capital of the World—Ayden, North Carolina

A BRIEF HISTORY OF SOUTHERN MANHOOD, continues

With so many entrepreneurs making money running moonshine during Prohibition, one Southern state levied a tax on bootleg whiskey. How could legislators fail to grasp the paradox of legally taxing illegal liquor? Today with drinking and driving an outlawed combination, many Southern states allow liquor stores to operate drive-through windows for the guy who wants to get goofed on the go.

How can a Southern Gentleman mourn the fall of the Confederacy and simultaneously pledge allegiance to the USA? How can a Good Old Boy buy a Dodge Ram truck without wondering: "dodge" or "ram," which is it? How? Chicken-fried logic, that's how. It's a regional thing like Brunswick stew or zydeco, and the boy-child learns it at the knees of skilled Southern samurai.

From crib to coffin, the Dixie boy's life is nothing but a prolonged attempt to snatch chaos from the jaws of order. Southern men disprove Darwin. Among other things, stubbornness, an exaggerated sense of honor, and taste for melodrama led to their defeat in 1865. But somehow those very traits assure the continuance of the Southern line. Manners, charm, and breeding far outweigh shooting straight, running fast, and being able to belly-crawl across a swamp. Southern evolution revolves around the survival of the zaniest.

How does such an ordered society manage to celebrate this continual behavioral free-for-all? Well, if something intolerable absolutely cannot be changed, shooed out of town, or shot down dead, Southerners will surrender. Using the old if-you-can't-beat-'em-join-'em rationale, they will not only accept the black sheep but welcome it into the flock, defend it, and brag about it so continually that they eventually forget any objections they may have harbored in the first place.

Sometimes unconventional behavior becomes so common as to go pretty much unnoticed. For example, a belle remembers how her father and one of his friends had fallen into the habit of eating lunch several times a week at the drugstore in their town. Often a third fellow, Tommy,

NICE THINGS ABOUT YANKEES

Live far away
Mind their own business
Archie Bunker
Pizza
Good tippers
Hilarious accents
No threat in beauty pageants
Good cop shows
The Buffalo Bills
The New York Mets

who was, as they say, "a little different" (meaning homosexual), joined them. One day Tommy slid onto his regular stool at the lunch counter looking dog tired, uncharacteristically rumpled, and badly in need of a shave. He ordered his usual ham sandwich and told the others that he'd just returned from New Orleans that very morning.

"Don't you think you're getting a little too old to be picking fights in New Orleans?" the belle's daddy teased.

Tommy laughed. "I'm too old to be *falling in love* in New Orleans, that's for damn sure."

That evening the belle's father related the lunch-counter conversation at home. "That's the first time in all these years I've known Tommy to be so open, so frank about being *that way.*" The belle and her sister thought this was hilarious and unbelievably naive of their dad. Her sister pointed out that Tommy had been wearing caftans and carrying a purse for years.

"Hmm." Their daddy pondered this. "I never thought much about that. Guess I figured that's just Tommy."

Dressing inappropriately sends a strong nonconformist message, but it's not the only way a Southern man asserts his crazy gene. In

IT'S HARD
TO THINK STRAIGHT WHEN
YOU'RE HOT

THEY SAY the Southern heat conspires against rational thought. Listen to what the heat did to one hot-blooded lawman.

The patrolman, one half of a two-man police force, had to work on Saturday night. He thought it'd be swift to take his date along as he dragged the main strip—two birds with one stone and all that. Things seemed peaceful on the beat, so about midnight, the law and the lady went parking. One thing led to another and they climbed into the backseat and squirmed out of their clothes. Mosquitoes distracted them from the lovemaking, so the lawman closed the doors to the car. Moments later he realized that the back doors on a blue-and-white police cruiser lock from the outside, where their clothes were. Both buck naked, the couple waited in the woods for twelve hours before the morning patrolman located them. By then the mood was gone.

A BRIEF HISTORY OF SOUTHERN MANHOOD, continues

Natchez, when a pillar of the community greets the mailman wearing a negligee, the letter carrier hardly bats an eye. It's the cross-dresser's liberal politics that keep the townsfolk scandalized. Neighbors lionized another Southern Gentleman for his originality after he underwent surgery to remove kidney stones, and then had the stones polished and set into an elegant brooch for his wife.

Crazy follows the Southern man like a hangover follows corn liquor. Southern Gentlemen grapple with oedipal complexes. Good Old Boys carry acute cases of homophobia. Practically all of them pick at scabs relating to the Lost Cause. Those are only a few of the name-brand neuroses running rampant in Dixie. Southern men have more ways to showcase their craziness than a bluetick hound has fleas. Some guys do loony things such as reenact Civil War battles over and over, refuse to wear pants, or barbecue roadkill and serve it with potato salad. Others go off on tangents babbling about out-there topics such as life on Mars, moving to New York City, or seeing Elvis at the mall.

Elvis himself was one crazy Good Old Boy. Graceland? Those jumpsuits? Please! Near Gafney, Georgia, some wacky Southern visionary constructed a giant peach on the side of the road. Not to be outdone, an eccentric postman in Texas spent much of his life building an entire museum dedicated to the orange. An artist in North Carolina created his unique living and studio space by refurbishing six salvaged school buses. His home is one big stationary field trip, which he graciously shares with twenty-five or so cats. And you can't find a bigger shrine to crazy than South of the Border, the roadside little Mexico on the North Carolina–South Carolina line. The guy who built that place reportedly pulled strings to have the interstate route altered so that more traveling families could experience his eccentricty.

But a man doesn't have to build something unusual to gain recognition as a certified Southern goofball. The most common manifestation of craziness in Southern manhood is found in neither word nor deed, but in a look. Remember Boo Radley from *To Kill a Mockingbird*? Or Roger Clinton? Ross Perot? Almost all Southerners, from time to time, get a downright weird sparkle in their eyes. That light can suggest nobody's home, or it can tip you off that somebody is home all right, and he's up to mischief.

Normal is difficult to achieve, because normal keeps changing all

1965   Alabama's Crimson Tide wins the national college football title.
1965   Atlanta dubs itself "The City Too Busy to Hate."

the time. Crazy is more consistent, and a hell of a lot easier to carry off. The Dixie boy noticed right away that the load with a few bricks missing totes much easier too. But don't go confusing eccentric with halfwitted. Crazy draws cheers in Dixie, but stupidity incites jeering. A guy who must take off his shoes, socks, and underwear to count to twenty-one is not prized by Southern society one bit, but a fellow who gets naked to pick up his dry cleaning is a community treasure.

Ask a serious, gray-bearded Freudian for his learned clinical opinion about Southern males. He'll likely puff his meerschaum and say, "Medically speaking? They're nuts."

That makes the pecan only the *second* most beloved nut in Dixie. While a belle can't make fruitcake out of the crazy men in her life, she can dine out on stories about them. God broke the mold and *then* made Southern men.

CHAPTER TEN

In High Cotton

Bringing Home the Bacon

WHEN ELVIS AND PRISCILLA PRESLEY'S daughter Lisa Marie was born, the cost of a standard hospital delivery in Memphis was $250.

I met the area doctor who first told Elvis the new baby was a girl. "I decided that if he gave out Cadillacs to the staff," the doctor recalled, "I wanted mine to be red."

No Coupe de Villes were issued though. And the absence of the King's legendary largesse started my doctor friend and others speculating. The physician in charge, they reckoned, must have presented an inflated bill for his services. Otherwise, Elvis would have awarded a showcase of fabulous prizes to the medical team just as surely as grits is groceries.

Several days after the birth, the mystery of the missing Cadillacs got even more puzzling. The Presleys' chief obstetrician—a Southern Gentleman in the grandest tradition—asked my doctor friend to cover a hospital shift for him. My friend agreed, "But only if you'll tell me how much you raked in on the Presley case, you sly dog."

"The regular rate, plus fifty dollars extra since we had to deal with the press," the gentlemanly gyno said flatly. "No reason to overcharge. That was all it was worth."

The Southern Gentleman's reluctance to collect extra cash might confuse corporate types in New York and Chicago. But it makes sense in

Memphis. And in Raleigh and Birmingham and Jackson, for that matter. Down South, a man's salary isn't his report card in life; his happiness is. Yankees may live to work, but Southerners work to live. "Young man in a hurry" isn't really a compliment around here. Dixie boys go to the office, or the factory, or the field every day, but they never forget that there's more to life than pushing a pencil or logging up sales calls on the cellular phone. They have fishing and TV and eating and getting laid to think about! And, well, if a fellow manages to sell a widget in between times, so much the better. As long as he doesn't have to unload it himself. For that, a Good Old Boy will charge extra, and a Southern Gentleman will say "Ah, never mind."

THE FRONT PORCH:
Poverty

*I*F AMERICANS *have been characterized as "people of plenty," Southerners have acquired a reputation as "folks of not enough." Small-time Southern farmers dealt with widespread poverty before, during, and after the Civil War. When the Great Depression gripped the nation during the 1930s, economically challenged Southerners hardly noticed a change. As bluesman Lonnie Johnson sang, "Hard times don't bother me. I was broke when it first started out."*

From poverty emerged many of the signature traits of Southern life. If it wasn't for hard times down South, there might be no grits, no hospitality, no tent revivals. Southern-styled poverty wed heartbreak and gave birth to the blues. Lazy Slim Jim sang the "Money Blues," and Blind Lemon Jefferson told of the "Broke and Hungry Blues." Even today the poor-but-proud lyrics of Dolly Parton and Loretta Lynn and Johnny Cash institutionalize and glamorize living hand-to-mouth in Dixie.

Southern poverty levels these days approach the national average, but there's hardly a person living below the Mason-Dixon who can't remember at least some kin psychologically scarred by poverty. A distinguished gentleman in Texas remembers his once-poor grandmother reusing paper plates. He holds a vivid picture of his aunt rinsing ice cubes and putting them back in the freezer.

Southerners who have survived hard times have a special way of looking at the world. "If you're not going to eat that Jell-O and the rest of that biscuit," a now rather affluent Southern man said while visiting a sick friend in the hospital, "I'll wrap it up and take it home to Pearl."

Old work-ethic axioms turn bass-ackward below the Mason-Dixon. The rich don't get richer and the poor don't get poorer. Instead, the rich get poor, the poor get rich, and few generations later they all do-si-do around again. A gold-digging belle shouldn't be fooled by a Southern Gentleman's song of old money. He might be singing about Confederate fortunes. A gal trolling for big bucks in Dixie should set her hook for a Good Old Boy with a fire in his belly and dollar signs dancing in his eyes.

Sometimes it just plain seems the Southern Gentleman goes out of his way to avoid riches, while the Good Old Boy runs after cash like a car-chasing dog. Nowhere is the difference between the Gentleman and the Good Old Boy more pronounced than when it comes to matters economic. Both types are like magnets for money; they're forever attracting or repelling it, depending on which way the good Lord polarized them.

The Gentleman repels it. He considers money to be vaguely dirty. Since he likely came by his robust balance sheet the easy way—congenitally—he values education and social position more than dollar signs. Oh, sure, he holds a job all right, but with a limp grip. He might deliver babies in Memphis, warehouse tobacco leaves in Winston-Salem, or plant peanuts in Plains. But no matter what his vocation, the Gentleman tackles it about half timidly. His true mission in life is signing checks, liberating himself from the burden of his bankroll.

The Good Old Boy, on the other hand, does his damnedest to acquire the taint of lucre. He believes dirt to be dirty, and money to be his ticket to a better life. Seeing as how he inherited an empty belly, he views wealth as his first step toward a big car, a country-club membership, a beauty queen, and a Rolex as big as a monkey's fist. He works hard and smart, selling real estate, replacing radiators, or coaching high-school football. But he can play lazy and stupid when it suits him too. Wall Street wheeler dealers never write the Good Old Boy venture capitalist off completely. As they say: "Whenever a Southerner says 'I'm just an old country boy'—watch your wallet!"

101 USES FOR KUDZU
#64—Prevents the South from rising again.

A BRIEF HISTORY OF SOUTHERN MANHOOD, continues

BEULAHLAND CASH CROPS

Indigo
Cotton
Tobacco
Fiction
Corn
Moonshine
Lumber
Beauty queens
Citrus
Sweet potatoes
Politicians
Catfish
Chickens
Pigs
Watermelons
Linebackers
Sugarcane
Televangelists

In some Southern states the age of marital consent may be fourteen, but your average Southern rich boy can't get his mitts on Grandpa's money until he turns twenty-one. And for good reason. The very day he realizes he has a fortune to tote around, he goes to work lightening his load. You know what they say: "Where there's a will, there's a way." But down here, where there's a will, there's a giveaway. Dry pine doesn't burn as fast as unearned wealth in the Southern Gentleman's pocket.

Robert E. Lee once said, "It's the stingy man who pays most in the end." You know the Southern Gentleman takes anything General Lee said to heart. That's part of the reason he believes it's a hundred times more blessed to give than to receive.

Take Uncle Daniel Ponder as a prime example of such blessedness. In Eudora Welty's novel *The Ponder Heart*, bighearted, open-handed Uncle Daniel's two favorite pastimes were visiting and making donations. That man loved happiness like some folks love tea. And he noticed that gift-giving brought a guaranteed smile to the face of both the philanthroper and the philanthropee.

I have a friend who periodically enjoys bouts of costly magnanimity that would do Uncle Daniel Ponder proud. My

1968 George Wallace runs for president on the American Independent ticket with running mate General Curtis Lemay.

133

friend's daddy one time arranged for him to assume management of a small grocery store. A local widow woman stopped in for the grand opening. She said, "I came to buy me a big old bill of groceries."

"Oh, no, ma'am," the gentleman proprietor replied. "Don't you buy your groceries here. I'm too high. Write down what you need and I'll pick it up over at Minimax and drop it by your house this evening." Do I even need to say it? He's much loved, but no longer in the grocery business.

Fellows cut from the same cloth as this former grocer enjoy "doing things"—crazy things like getting drunk and buying a hound dog a first-class airline ticket to Memphis, getting drunk and moving an old house across town, or getting drunk and doing most anything imaginative. About the only things a Southern Gentleman does not like to do is take money from other people and sweat to make a buck.

The Gentleman is not contemptuous of work. It's more like he's indifferent to it. He just can't see allowing some silly job to cut into his enjoyment of life and pleasure in humankind. And when all is said and done? Much more gets said than done.

Depending on his mood, a gentleman in Dallas describes his occupation variously as "romeo, rogue, raconteur, or post-modern bon vivant." More conventional occupations favored by the Southern Gentleman include country lawyer, small-town doctor, and, occasionally, politician. Really any job where he can sit around and jaw sounds good to him, but some careers stand out as more appealing than others. Subject in a sleep-research laboratory, full-time Nielsen viewer, or talent scout for a fashion-modeling agency would be among the positions listed in the Southern Gentleman's All-Time Good Job Hall of Fame.

EUPHEMISMS FOR "NEEDY"

Sucking the hind tit.
Too broke to pay attention.
Our house was so small, we had to go outside to change our minds.
My folks were so busted, I had a pet hookworm.
We were so poor we'd eat apricots, drink water, and watch our stomachs swell just for fun.
Rubbing nickels together to make a dime.
Squeezing a dollar till the eagle shits.
Economically challenged.

A BRIEF HISTORY OF SOUTHERN MANHOOD, continues

Sometime-Louisianan John James Audubon hit on a pretty good scam. He got paid to sit in a duck blind, look at birds, and then draw their pictures. Craig Claiborne of Mississippi has fashioned a fine career eating good food. That's just about your average Gentleman's idea of heaven. The only way it could be better would be if he could get paid to sample high-calorie cooking in topless bars. "Now there's a job!"

My daddy worked in a bank and was briefly mayor of our town. He once confessed that neither post was what he really wanted to do. His true calling? "I've always thought it'd be nice to get up every day and water the grass in the town square."

Since the Southern Gentleman commonly passes most days in the shade being actively charming, getting paid to tell stories ranks among the most honest ways to make a living. Aristocratic Southerners with no money dine out on stories—literally. Writers in the Larry Brown, Harry Crews, and Walker Percy vein go to the office, spin yarns about their crazy kinfolk, and draw a paycheck for it. Young men too scrawny to play football, too bashful to preach, too honest to run for Congress buy word processors. They say more people write books in Mississippi than read them. There's a good chance that anybody firing a gun in Dixie will wing a writer. Fiction, like cotton, is a popular Southern staple consumed heavily around the world.

The Southern Gentleman unable to wring a living wage out of storytelling might fall back on gardening as a profession. Big-time gardening, or "planting" as the unabashedly pretentious say, has been the linchpin of the region's economy for centuries. Dixie boys have traditionally found a thrill in coaxing plants out of the ground—tomatoes, azaleas, cotton. It's in their blood. Even the most metropolitan transplanted Southerner keeps the weeds away from the geraniums in his flower bed, or nurses nasturtiums in a window box, or at the very least

BUMPER STICKER

PLEASE TAILGATE —I NEED THE MONEY.

waters a fern in a terra-cotta pot from time to time. My neighbor plants ten different kinds of cotton in his tiny front yard just to remind him of his roots. He tends the plots for hours every day, enticing joggers to stop and gawk and visit awhile.

Any job where he's not likely to strain his back appeals to the Southern Gentleman. And if it doesn't pay much, so what? Down South there's no disgrace in delinquent bills. As a Winston-Salem attorney puts it, "It was bad form to have money after the War." To this very day, shame follows those families who failed to burn their crops before Sherman got to them. As far as some folks are concerned, fortunes made trading with the carpetbaggers still stink to high heaven. Poverty has dignity in the South, where defeat remains more glorious and glamorous than victory. The standard-issue Southern Gentleman possesses a hereditary predisposition for lost causes *and* lost wages. That's why he chooses to emphasize breeding and manners rather than net worth.

Who you are may no longer take precedence over what you do, but around here it still outweighs what you have. An entrepreneurial Good Old Boy in Texas once said of a threadbare Gentleman friend: "His family made their money so long ago that they've forgotten how to earn it."

Some patrician stars of the Southern social scene haven't written a good check in years. Poverty, like nuts in the family tree, shouts aristocracy. In Charleston, old families enjoy recalling how Ted Turner almost wasn't invited to join the Carolina Yacht Club. To the uninitiated, Turner would seem amply qualified—his media fortune is second generation, and he skippered his yacht to victory in the America's Cup. But old Charlestonians refer to him as part of the "money talks" crowd. They quickly point out that big bucks do not guarantee inclusion into Southern society.

Which is better: (A) old blood and no money, or (B) new blood and new money?

A DIXIE BOY'S REASONS NOT TO GO TO WORK

Sick
Mother sick
Tired
Fish biting
Raining
Too hot
Traffic jam
No clean shirts
Forgot
Don't feel like it

A BRIEF HISTORY OF SOUTHERN MANHOOD, continues

If you answered A, you're a Southern Gentleman; B means you're probably a Good Old Boy.

The phrase "more blue than green" refers to blue blood and greenbacks. "Had money once" means a century ago. And "new money" means they made it after the War and are likely still considered carpetbaggers, as common as clay, by some snooty old-timers. In the lingo of Southern heraldry, "signer" refers to one whose ancestors signed the town charter and who more than likely today signs credit slips and loan applications.

"Don't ever give me a million dollars. It'd come between us." That's the view of the Southern Gentleman. But the Good Old Boy might take another tack: "Hand me a million," wink, wink, "and I'll take care of it for y'all." He's not above skimming the gravy off the grits. When you go out to see him on business, go naked—that way you won't feel the cold coming back.

It's not like the Good Old Boy is greedy. He just puts first things first. And that means himself and his family. Take the small-business owner

who sadly informed his employees one day that he had been forced to cut their salaries. "You know, with my daughter in school in Switzerland and the new summer place out at Hilton Head and all." Another fellow had to eliminate his staff's Christmas bonuses one year because his wife had gone and bought two fur coats and twenty-five microwave ovens as gifts for her extended family. Around here when people talk about a "poor" Good Old Boy, they might just be talking about a guy whose baby has to sleep in the box the color TV came in.

While the modern Southern Gentleman clings to the glory of the Old South, the Good Old Boy gets all excited about the promise of the New. The Gentleman remains a depository of philanthropic urges; the Good Old Boy bulges with moneymaking schemes. He figures, "If the hogs don't come when you yell soooie, holler something else."

The longest battle in Southern history wasn't Vicksburg but *is* the ongoing skirmish about progress. Do we dig in our heels and hope the Old South rises again? Or do we go ahead and build a zillion minimalls and resign ourselves to the fact that the Yankees who come down to enjoy the year-round golf and sunshine will bring plenty of money to spend?

In the early 1980s, some developers planned to put up a shopping mall near the Manassas battlefield in Virginia. Right away Southern Gentlemen went to ranting and raving about the lack of respect for tradition. Good Old Boys, meanwhile, began working on architectural drawings and financial plans. The Southern Gentlemen, bless their hearts, can't help being haunted by images of Atlanta burning. The

SOUTHERN GUYS WITH GOOD JOBS

Fred Couples—*Golfer*
Jerry Jones—*Owner of the Dallas Cowboys*
Craig Claiborne—*Food Critic*
Lewis Grizzard—*Professional Storyteller*
Dale Earnhardt—*Stock-car Driver*
Richard Guy and Rex Holt—*Beauty Pageant Producers*
Jimmy Swaggart—*Flamboyant TV Preacher*
Strom Thurmond—*Outspoken Politician*
Colonel Tom Parker—*King Maker*
Bill Clinton—*President of the United States*
Roger Clinton—*Baby Brother to the President of the United States*

A BRIEF HISTORY OF SOUTHERN MANHOOD, continues

Good Old Boys learned a lesson from the fire too: Invest in buckets.

One slick Good Old Boy in Florida turned death into do-re-mi. After learning that he was dying of a brain tumor, he took out classified ads. For $20, the ads promised, this guy would deliver messages to loved ones on the Other Side. And he offered a money-back guarantee. What could clients do if he didn't deliver? How could they prove it? Savvy Dixie boys hang on to a simple, portable business philosophy that they can apparently pack up and take right into the next life: "Don't sweat the petty things, and don't pet the sweaty things."

Besides being natural-born entrepreneurs, Good Old Boys not blessed with innovative ideas usually have mastered the fine art of buttering up the boss. The best way to get ahead is to have a good idea. The second best way is to kiss the butt of the guy in front of you. As one Good Old Boy noted when he went to work for a big corporation: "He promised me six digits. I should've known I'd have to suck the first one."

Your average Good Old Boy was born to vend—anything. He sells folks what they want to buy regardless of the goods in his sample case. "I'm not pushing Bibles, ma'am. I'm offering redemption at a low, low price." Since he can easily finesse a wart off a witch's nose, talking money out of a prospective customer is nothing but a walk in the park for the Willie Starbucks of the world. "Vacuum cleaner? Why, sir, this your ticket to the future. Welcome to the Space Age." When he hits a dry spell, the Southern salesman tries to be philosophical: "Even a blind hog gets an acorn sooner or later."

The Good Old Boy also prefers to be his own boss. Owning a small business fits his personality just fine. Coaching—now there's something he might think of doing if he ever gets bored with making money. When I read about an opening for a municipal squirrel hunter in some small

HEROES

OF

THE

PEN

William Faulkner
Willie Morris
Walker Percy
Lewis Grizzard
John Grisham
Tennessee Williams
John Shelton Reed
Larry Brown
Roy Blount, Jr.
Shelby Foote
Harry Crews
Alex Haley
Dave Barry
Truman Capote
Dan Jenkins

1973 Alabama wins another national football championship.
1974 Hank Aaron of the Atlanta Braves hits his 715th home run.

town in North Carolina, I knew Good Old Boys all over the South were already copying résumés.

Instead of writing books, the Good Old Boy is more apt to tell his stories in a country song. The past recurs as a perennial favorite topic at The Grand Old Opry. Crooners remember the old days before sharecroppers' shacks and cotton fields gave way to skyscrapers and business deals. The thought of skyscrapers replacing sharecroppers' shacks might depress the temperamental Southern Gentleman, but the gung-ho Good Old Boy couldn't be more tickled by it. Why? He grew up in a shotgun shack and doesn't miss it one bit. Heck, he also probably owns a piece of the skyscraper.

That's the craziest part of the social economics of the South. The Good Old Boy's sons grow up to be Gentlemen, and the other way around. Poverty and wealth, industriousness and laziness, seem to occur in alternating generations down Dixie way. Daddy builds a business, and forty years later Sonny files Chapter 11.

An acquaintance who operates a medium-size company near the Louisiana/Mississippi line remembers pushing a plow through his family's fields. "I'll never forget the hot, hot day when I decided that there had to be a better way to make a living, and that I was going to find it." He did find it. And now that he's built himself a bank account, that Good Old Boy bemoans the fact that his sons will never know the farming way of life so important to his identity. "Those boys of mine—shoot! They'll never know diddly about hard work."

A few years back some bureaucrats in Washington published a study calling the South the "nation's number-one economic problem." Did Southerners worry? No way. Those Yankee pencil-pushers just didn't understand Dixie ingenuity, that's all. The Southern way of business sometimes involves selling Bibles at a loss and hoping to make up for it in volume.

So what about those missing Cadillacs? I asked my doctor friend in Memphis: Why did Elvis turn stingy?

Elvis was a Good Old Boy, my friend finally decided, and a Good Old Boy doesn't overpay. I wondered, "Do you believe he's still alive?"

The doctor considered this for a minute or two and said, "If he is, you can be damned sure he owns stock in those tabloids."

CHAPTER ELEVEN

Buckling Some Swash

Semper Fi, *Y'all*

H E'S FASTER THAN A SPEEDING NASCAR, stronger than the 'Bama offensive line. He jumps to conclusions in a single bound. *He's Captain Confederacy!*

You think I'm making this up, but I'm not. I recently ran across a comic book about the ultimate Dixie warrior. He lives in a tantalizing, what-if universe, a present-day South where the sword was passed the other way at Appomattox. In this contemporary Confederate States of America the national motto crows "Progress is our middle name." Texas and Louisiana have seceded from the Confederate Union—boy, does that sound odd!—and become independent nations. James Dean lives. The top-rated breakfast television program is *Good Morning Dixie.* And the president? It's President Lee, of course, a female descendant of the first President Lee who freed the slaves right after the Rebs sent the Yanks running north with their tails tucked.

By day, Captain Confederacy is a mild-mannered actor. But just let him see somebody doing bad, and he pulls on his Stars-and-Bars leotard and pops open a can of kickass.

How'd he get so superhuman? Let me explain. In the first install-ment, the Confederate Bureau of Investigation scientists engineered a hero serum capable of making normal men "ten times as strong and half as smart." Instead of going ahead and selling the super juice as-is to the World Wrestling Federation, the evil genius behind the strength formu-

T H E   F R O N T   P O R C H :
Boys' Clubs

*E*VEN THOUGH *they embrace the idea of themselves as Rebels, Southern men are much more likely to join up than to secede. From the Rotarians to the KKK, Dixieland bulges with all-male secret societies and social clubs and coffee klatches. South-central L.A. doesn't have a thing on the South-central USA when it comes to gang membership.*

Joining a lodge is a more popular manly Southern hobby than Elvis impersonating because a fellow gets an excuse to spout mystic hocus-pocus and strut around in outlandish outfits and to do the occasional good deed for the community, all for the price of membership.

The Good Old Boy has got secret societies like the Masons and the Knights of Pythias, where the membership is well known but the mystics can't be divulged. "Ooops! I accidentally slipped you the secret handshake. Now I'm going to have to kill you." Business clubs like the Lions, the Rotarians, and the Kiwanis are big down South too. Members of those organizations meet at lunchtime, pig out on a steam-table buffet, and discuss new ways to make money. Some fellows belong to flag-waving societies like the Sons of the Confederacy or the Sons of the American Revolution. Then there are scads of all-male social clubs—bachelor's organizations and college frats—which seem dedicated to landing members dates with Southern belles. Other all-boy clubs—like the St. Cecilia Society in Charleston or Idlewild in Dallas—seem mostly about ensuring the continuance of a snobbish status quo, keeping the "in" crowd in from one generation to the next.

Charles Reagan Wilson wrote about one colorful joiner in Mississippi whose fraternal activities included "secretary of the Knights of Pythias for fourteen years, Great Sachem of the Red Men of Mississippi and a member of the Woodmen of the World, the Elks, the Mystic Shrine, a Knight Templar and Thirty-Second Degree Mason." His membership dues alone would feed a family of four for a year.

The military remains the ultimate Southern fraternity. Well, perhaps the penultimate. It's a safe bet that a Southern Gentleman elected to the U.S. Senate has to resist a powerful urge to list it on his tax return as "fraternal organization."

A BRIEF HISTORY OF SOUTHERN MANHOOD, continues

la worked the "half as smart" kinks out of it and injected this unemployed actor. The plan was to have him star in government propaganda films. The CBI operatives thought the good people of Dixie City needed "a hero to identify with. Someone to direct their sympathies when he fights against terrorists and foreigners."

A true Southern superhero has to be a rebel or there's no future for the comic book. So sure enough, after a few turns for the propaganda cameras in issue #1, Captain Confederacy breaks away from his government handlers and starts busting heads free-lance. Along with his big-breasted, Southern belle sidekick Miss Dixie (she also got a shot of the super serum), the Captain goes around ferreting out Yankee spies who've infiltrated the Confederate government.

I'm surprised that the *Captain Confederacy* comics series hasn't caught on like Goo Goo Clusters around here. If given half a chance, the Captain and Miss Dixie could squeeze Superman and Wonder Woman out of young Southerners' hearts in a Memphis minute. From childhood, Southern boys love a good fight—picking it, watching it, participating in it, and especially talking about it after it's over. Call it a martial spirit, bellicosity, or just plain old blood lust. Whatever you name it, the Southerner's penchant for violence comes with the territory and has been a part of the fabric of Beulahland life for a long, long time. Alexis de Tocqueville reported a century or so ago that the male Southerner was "passionately fond of hunting and war." Passionately fond, my hind foot! I'd say he's plain crazy for bone crushing and bloodletting as long as it's for a good cause. The Southern cause.

You can't drive old Dixie down for long. Maybe the South embraces violence because it was wilderness around here until not that long ago. Or it could be that Yankee propagandists dreamed up this image of the hardscrabble South as

101 USES FOR KUDZU

89—Covers the junk piled in the yard.

1976   Ted Turner's superstation goes on the air.
1976   Dixie boy Jimmy Carter becomes president.

143

a way to rationalize why it took them four years to subdue what everybody agrees was an inferior army. Whatever the reason, in Dixieland men take stands. Gentlemen spar. Good Old Boys brawl. Legislators filibuster. Shoot, even banjo players duel. The South is America's Sparta. Every Southerner sees himself as Captain Confederacy. His

HEROES OF THE SWORD

Robert E. Lee
Stonewall Jackson
Audie Murphy
Oliver North
The Tuskegee Airmen
Pierre G. T. Beauregard
Norman Schwarzkopf
William Tecumseh Sherman
Andrew Jackson

A BRIEF HISTORY OF SOUTHERN MANHOOD, continues

patriotism and pugilism have become so tied up together, he even snarls with a drawl. Belles have learned to love and expect that fighting spirit.

As a Southern congressman once told an interviewer: "We've got to have militaristic sumbitches like me so smart-asses like you can shoot off your mouth whenever you want."

I once met a former marine from Mississippi. He said that he couldn't remember the exact percentage, but that "a whole bunch" of the total Marine Corps comes from the South. "Just to give you an idea how Southern the Corps is," he said, "when I was in boot camp we spent twelve hours learning about the M-1 rifle and thirty hours being drilled in honor, tradition, and history."

Turns out that leatherneck knew his stuff. Sociologists have done studies that show that men with Southern affiliations—birth, school, or marriage—are represented disproportionately in the U.S. military. Before Pearl Harbor, Texans went around bragging that the government introduced the draft especially to keep them from filling up the armed forces. Young Southerners train for war even in peacetime. The Citadel in South Carolina and the Virginia Military Institute remain two of most revered institutions in the South, and the last two state-supported schools to let go of the all-male military tradition. Forget the Rotarians, the Lions, and Kiwanians. The army is the ultimate Southern fraternity, the most high-stakes hunting trip of all. Spit and polish, honor and patriotism, picking fights and kicking butt, form a big part of the whole idea of Dixie manhood.

Every now and then Dixie machismo crosses the line to masochism. If a Southerner acknowledges pain after anything less than a gunshot wound or a gelding, he's considered a wimp. "Yellow" means the same thing as un-American, un-Southern, un-manly. A big boy doesn't cry, at least not as a result of physical pain. He tears up when the band plays "Dixie," when he sees his son run for a touchdown or his daughter crowned homecoming queen. If hedonism is the goal of a good Southern life, stoicism offers the means of attaining it. The stoic Southern Gentleman wants nothing in this world so much as to be heroic.

There's an old saying that a Southern man is always a polite gentleman, until he's angry enough to kill you. If the Southern belle has raised eyelash batting to an art form, then the Southern Gentleman has elevated fightpicking to a science. If the Gentleman's fighting style brings to mind Errol Flynn, the Good Old Boy's combat conjures images

TO BLUBBER
OR NOT TO BLUBBER?

The Southern man will cry when . . .
 . . . *he hears "Dixie."*
 . . . *his son runs for a touchdown.*
 . . . *his daughter gets crowned Homecoming Queen.*
 . . . *his mama cries.*
 . . . *he gets married.*
 . . . *his team loses a big game.*
 . . . *his dog gets a thorn in the paw.*
 . . . *he hears "I Stopped Loving Her Today."*
The Southern man will not cry when . . .
 . . . *his team wins a big game.*
 . . . *he declares bankruptcy.*
 . . . *he drops a microwave oven on his foot.*
 . . . *he breaks a limb.*
 . . . *he sees a sad movie.*
 . . . *he hears "The Battle Hymn of the Republic."*
 . . . *he kills a deer.*
 . . . *he gets shot.*

146

A BRIEF HISTORY OF SOUTHERN MANHOOD, continues

of Yosemite Sam. He'll say, "I'm fixing to skin you alive, tan your hide, knock you naked, wipe the floor with your raggedy ass, rip your head off, and—" The hype always oversells the main event.

The Southern warrior likes his sparring the way he likes his sex—with a little creative foreplay before getting down to business. Where an irate Midwesterner curses an adversary concisely—"you son of a bitch"—a pissed-off Good Old Boy puts his heart and soul into trash talking. He modifies the hell out of an insult, drawling "You yellow-bellied, low-down, sorry-ass, no-account, chicken-shit sumbitch." Sometimes before serving up his special-recipe knuckle sandwich, the Southerner might set the table by composing a custom-made, personalized pearl of unkindness. "Buddy, if brains was dynamite, you couldn't blow your nose." Or "Listen, Jack, you about as close to smart as a frog is to a hippie hairdo."

Before a fight, the efficient Northerner wastes no energy or time. He threatens only his immediate foe. Not the Southern man. That son of a gun slings gibes not only at his enemy, but he also talks down all of the villain's kin, his ancestors, and his dog, sometimes in a single masterpiece of denigration. "Your daddy don't know come here from sic 'em, and that damn mutt of yours looks about as smart as a bag of crap."

When forced to abbreviate his provocation, the Southerner makes it a stout one. "I'd cut you down, but diarrhea don't slice."

From what you hear on the news, it seems like the basic Yankee tough guy likely resorts to violence over lost or damaged property. He might slit another person's throat to recover a stolen stereo, for example. More often than not, the Southerner will let theft slide. He makes a fist only to avenge impugned honor—the good name of his family, his state,

BUMPER STICKER

THIS CAR INSURED BY SMITH AND WESSON

and, as he sees it, the integrity of the entire South. Thing is, the Dixie boy's honor antenna picks up an insult like a dog's ears prick up for a high-pitched whistle. He's got his gun loaded and is out the door before most mere mortals even realize that somebody, somewhere has dropped a gauntlet.

After a brawl comes the Southerner's postscript, the replay. A Yankee walks away from a three-minute row and forgets about it; the Dixie boy dusts himself off after the same spat and talks about it for the next fifty years. With each retelling, the Southerner's victory becomes more decisive, his cause more virtuous, and his valor more spectacular, no matter what the actual outcome of the skirmish.

All this Monday-morning quarterbacking unwinds in the most eloquently euphemistic terms. The Southerner will wax poetic about how he dotted this lowlife's eye or cleaned that so-and-so's plow. But the Southern Gentleman reserves his best battle ruminations for remembrances of the Big One: "the War of Yankee

BEST NOT MENTIONED

Boy George
Notre Dame
Richard Simmons
U. S. Grant
Dr. Pritikin
Teddy Kennedy
ACLU
Torvill and Dean
Thelma and Louise
Giorgio Armani
The Brady Bill
RuPaul

A BRIEF HISTORY OF SOUTHERN MANHOOD, *continues*

Aggression" or "the War for Southern Independence," or even "the War Between the Good Guys and the Bad Guys."

Why not the just "the Civil War?" Because—"Those damn Yankees coming down here and burning up our country"—the Southerner sees nothing "civil" about it.

As one present-day Southerner bragged to a New Jersey–American: "Shucks, we could have whupped y'all with cornstalks."

FIGHTING WORDS

hick
yokel
hillbilly
cracker
redneck
bumpkin
Communist
your mama . . .
White Trash
Yankee

1981   Jeff Barber wins the National Tobacco Spitting Contest in Raleigh, Mississippi, with a world-record heave of 33 feet, 7 1/2 inches.

"Ha!" the Yank replied. "Then why didn't youse go ahead and do it?"

" 'Cause y'all wouldn't fight with cornstalks, that's why."

Dixie boys who want the South to stay Southern sometimes get blamed with continuing to fight the Civil War. Once, when a Southern governor and his wife went to a party at the Nixon White House, an aide briefed them on protocol dictating that each governor be introduced in the order that his state entered the union. The Southern governor asked in all seriousness, "Which time?"

The folk heroes of the Northeast might be shrewd capitalists—Rockefeller, Getty, Forbes. But the South's heroes are soldiers—Lee, Jackson, Schwarzkopf—sometimes shrewd, but always honorable and brave.

The Dixie boy never runs away from a fight. He runs toward it, and has for at least a century. When the Confederacy called for 100,000 army volunteers, so many eager young recruits arrived for induction that one-third of them had to be sent home. The Confederate generals assumed that one Rebel could easily whip the tarnation out of twenty Yankees. Gentlemen, they reckoned, could fight more valiantly than rabble. But alas, the Southern strategists turned out to be wrong. Even good breeding, lovely manners, and dashing uniforms couldn't save a lost cause.

The Lost Cause—scholars really do use capital letters for this—remains a vividly pungent but glorious memory around here. In the Dixie boy's mind the whole episode has evolved into a grand, knightly quest. The righteous may not triumph in battle, he concedes, but the righteous will endure in the end. By God, the South will rise again. And again, and again, and again.

William Faulkner once said of the South, "The past is not dead. It isn't even past." Around here the past seeps into the present like smoke from a barbecue grill. Civil War buffs collect guns, subscribe to special magazines, buy historically accurate lead soldiers, go to conventions.

TOUGH, NOT CRUEL

No matter how many nails he eats for breakfast, the quality Good Old Boy never bullies. Toughness is valued, cruelty is not. A small-town ag teacher learned this lesson the hard way when the school district fired him for allowing a student to castrate a pig with his teeth.

A BRIEF HISTORY OF SOUTHERN MANHOOD, continues

FORGET, HELL!

W. G. Harding of Tennessee vowed not to shave until the South won the war. He was buried in 1886 with a beard down to his waist.

There's a guy in Washington state who has built a recording career singing songs he's written about the Civil War. The 97th Regimental String Band in Florida does the same. But the most obsessed hobbyists play dress-up with a vengeance.

Nearly 150 years after Lee's surrender, hundreds of grown men gather each July to replay the battle of Gettysburg. These boys don't simply mime the shooting parts of the skirmish either. They camp out on the hillside, eat old-time battle rations, and sing "Dixie" until the break of dawn. Then, just before they charge, all decked out in their gray-and-gold battle uniforms, they repeat the same prayers for victory their ancestors mumbled so long ago. Every year the good guys lose again, but always with the utmost grace and honor.

Fellows with Civil War hangups remind themselves that bad things sometimes happen to good people. They cite General Robert E. Lee as proof. Dixie venerates Lee and other veterans like apostles. At Stone Mountain in Georgia, craftsmen blasted likenesses of the region's holy trinity—Lee, Jefferson Davis, Stonewall Jackson—into rock as eternal examples of manly courage. Some call the shrine "the South's Mount Rushmore," but really it's more like Dixie's Wailing Wall or a magnolia-land Mecca. In the South, soldiers are saints, that's all. And our boys to this very day jump at the chance to become martyrs for a glorious cause.

James Dickey reportedly once said that he's more proud of being a Southerner than of being an American. Not all Good Old Boys would go that far, but most of them are happy that they haven't had to choose between those loyalties in a long time. Among the desert tribesmen of the Middle East there's a saying: "I against my brothers. I and my brothers against my cousins. I, my brothers, and my cousins against the world." Well, that sort of sums up the Southerner's loyalty to the United States. The Dixie boy sides with the Reb against the Yank, but he stands with the Reb and the Yank against the Commie.

A Southern World War II veteran I know talked down Yankees constantly until the day two Japanese businessmen showed up in his golf foursome. "I can't put my finger on it," he said, "but I was leery of those guys carrying sticks."

And when the Southerner walks softly and carries a big stick, the stick usually has a firing pin and a trigger. Studies show that about 65 percent of Southerners pack heat, as compared with 41 percent of non-Southerners. I heard a story about an urban Southerner who drives to work with a loaded pistol tucked under the front seat of his sedan because "People are just so *mean* these days."

Worried sick that the Democrats in Washington planned to disarm America, a gentleman in Dallas gave pistols to everybody on his Christmas list one year. A guy in Georgia got drunk and fired his piece into his closet by accident. Now each of his suits has a neatly darned bullet hole in the jacket. In Florida, a sober fellow angry at his wife opened fire into his wardrobe too. He drilled holes in his dress shirts. Not to imply that Southerners are closet gun lovers. Far from it. They're out and they're proud.

When state legislators learned that more Texas citizens died one year from gunfire than from car wrecks, they knew it was time for action. So they introduced a bill to raise the speed limit.

Around here, a young whippersnapper gets his first gun before he can color inside the lines of his coloring book. Each successive step up in firepower represents a coming-of-age ritual. A little fellow gets a BB gun for his fifth birthday. With it, he obliterates frogs and sparrows and annoys the heck out of dogs. My brother accidentally winged the garbage man with his BB gun. That meant he had to wait a few extra years before getting a rifle.

Once a boy owns a .22, he quits gunning down garden amphibians and goes after rabbits and squirrels. About the time he starts shaving—maybe a little bit before if he's ballistically precocious—the young warrior graduates to a small-caliber shotgun and begins taking doves and quails out of their misery. By the time he's driving drunk and kissing girls, the Dixie boy owns a deer rifle. Big, phallic, and powerful, there's nothing like it to reassure him he's a man.

As he grows older, the Southern soldier of fortune will hang a gun rack in his pickup truck. He'll slap a GUNS DON'T KILL, PEOPLE DO bumper sticker on all his family's cars. When he becomes more successful in business, he'll spend big bucks collecting Civil War–era weaponry. With his hunting buddies he'll dress up in a camouflage outfit and travel to con-

1982   Bear Bryant retires after 323 football victories.

vention-center gun shows, where weapon aficionados convene to covet knives, survival gear, and ammo. Southern men just love to play GI Joe. In Houston, a paramilitary-themed nightclub—complete with an army green stretcher as a buffet table, bartenders in camo, waitresses in bandoliers, and restrooms labeled "latrine"—did a booming business for a while; "booming" becomes, of course, the key word.

"I think they're from somewhere around here," a Southerner said of her new neighbors.

"Why's that?" her friend asked. "Do they speak with Southern accents?"

"In a way. The other night when the husband didn't like what was on TV, he just got his gun and shot out the television set."

KA–BOOM! The most Southern accent of all.

When he's not in uniform, Captain Confederacy uses a pistol sometimes too. I've only seen a couple of issues of the comic, but I gather that the one thing guaranteed to get Captain Confederacy and Miss Dixie steamed is the mistreatment of African-Americans, or rather African-Confederates. As I said, this is a what-if genre.

If you are creating a perfect Southern world, you might as well go all the way, right? In a country where *Good Morning Dixie* airs at breakfast, *Hee Haw* and *The Dukes of Hazzard* probably rule in prime time. Could be that Madame President Lee succeeded law-and-order President George Wallace, who took over after the eight-term reign of Huey P. Long. Hank Williams, Jr., just might be logging up the globe-trotting miles as the CSA secretary of state; his policy papers set to music top the country charts. Colonel Tom Parker could well be Brigadier General Parker by now, head of the Confederate armed forces.

Chances are in these what-if Confederate states, marrying your cousin is not only accepted but promoted since fewer name changes cut down on the bureaucracy and reduce government. The nation's number-one fast food restaurant, McChitlins, serves free collards and passes out little condiment packets of syrup and cream gravy. Cars built at the GM plant in Richmond now come with factory-installed glass-pack mufflers and gun racks. Mandatory prayer takes up half the public school day, and football practice takes up the rest.

Meanwhile, people in Pennsylvania and Massachusetts sit around talking about the good old days, promising that, someday, the North will rise again.

CHAPTER TWELVE

The Kindness of Strangers

To the Manner Born

I HAVE A FRIEND WHO IS SOMETHING OF AN expert on all things Southern. A fine Southern Gentleman his ownself, he thinks he's figured out just what makes Dixie boys so dang deluxe. His equation has four elements—kinship, religion, food, and the military.

Recently, when driving through Alabama, he zoomed past a billboard advertisement for a Chevrolet dealership. It bore the slogan IT'S A GOOD CAR, PAW-PAW! A few miles on down the road he pulled into a diner—or "café," as they say in Alabama—for a bite to eat. Inside, seated at the counter, he fell into quite a debate with a local Baptist minister and others about current events. The discussion was interrupted when a young local boy dropped in to say good-bye before leaving to join the marines.

Now, within thirty minutes, my friend had come across everything that he believes makes a Southern man Southern. Kinship—IT'S A GOOD CAR, PAW-PAW! Food—at the counter he'd been torn between the fried chicken and the ham, and finally ordered a little of both. Religion—as a Baptist, the preacher wore no collar, but he'd included his holy credentials in his "how do." Military—the boy boarding the bus for boot camp had never been outside Alabama before.

Even though he's an expert, my friend overlooked something key. The final—and from the female perspective the most important—ingredient in the recipe for delicious Southern manhood? Nice manners.

The South doesn't hold a monopoly on civility, but the Dixieland man believes that along with his drawl and his penchant for fighting and romance, his courtly manners assure that his Southernness will never seep away.

Southern people want to think the best of each other. Around here "ma'am" and "sir" replace "buddy" and "lady." They aren't terms of servility, but just matters of common courtesy. Next time you cool your heels in a traffic jam in Manhattan or Los Angeles, listen to how many

THE FRONT PORCH:
Hospitality

*C*OME ON IN, *take your shoes off. Y'all come back now, you hear? Southern hospitality is one positive Dixie myth. All that stuff about racism and incest and illiteracy and dirt-eating shines an ugly and false light on Southern living. The rumors about Southern hospitality, on the other hand, have not been greatly exaggerated. If anything, they've been understated. Southern hospitality isn't a quaint fiction. Friends, it's a fact.*

Something about the South, maybe the leafy canopy or the sticky heat, just invites nesting. Long ago, when the region was mostly wilderness, Southerners charged itinerant strangers for room and board. But a simple letter of introduction made a stranger a friend, a member of the family. Today not even door-to-door salesmen get screen doors slammed in their faces down South. Anybody with good manners is welcomed as a friend.

I know a Southern Gentleman who'd close up his office if a pair of Mormon preachers came by. He'd put up that little cardboard clock with the BE BACK AT . . . *sign on it, and take the ministers out to the country club for lunch and introduce them to all his friends.*

Southern parents take in their children's college friends, they invite the gardener's daughter to live in the garage apartment, or encourage Aunt Sister to come visit at Christmas and stay on until Easter. All the South loves a stray—even a stray with a Brooklyn accent.

All the talk around here about damn Yankees is mostly just talk. A Southerner doesn't want to disappoint, so he gladly plays the part of Lost Cause knight when the occasion arises. But let a reasonably friendly Yankee knock on a Good Old Boy's door, and within minutes he'll push a drink into that Yankee's hand and regale him with stories about the good old days. Southern hospitality offers the Dixie boy a chance to show a visitor how Southern he is and to advertise what's so great about the South.

A BRIEF HISTORY OF SOUTHERN MANHOOD, continues

angry drivers honk their horns. Compare that with the number honking in Nashville or Atlanta, where nice people consider drawing attention to oneself in a crowd to be rude.

Social graces have been valued as a manly virtue around here for quite a spell. After the War, a courtly code of conduct was all many Southerners had left. In a region of general poverty, manners alone elevated "nice" people from riffraff. Early in this century some forward-thinking capitalists planned to open a hotel in Washington, Georgia. "It'll be good for business," civic boosters said. "Stir up some commerce." One stodgy pillar of the community didn't see the situation in the same light as the others. He concluded that any gentleman visiting on business could stay at his house, and that anyone who wasn't a gentleman should be encouraged to pass on through.

Good manners are almost a genetic trait in the South, passed down from generation to generation like heart disease. King James I of England once remarked, "I can make a lord, but only God Almighty can make a gentleman." God Almighty or a Southern mother. In junior high school, a boy in my class got a good birching when he failed to hold the door for a female teacher. "I know your mama would just be sick," the principal told him before swinging the switch, "and ashamed."

My mother always insisted that my brother stand when a woman walked up to our table at the country club. If ever he forgot, he caught a Ferragamo in the shin. Many a Sunday morning he stood there and watched his chicken get cold while some old bird chattered away with the latest gossip. An older gentleman demonstrated how as a boy he tried to fool his mother by just raising his shoulders instead of standing. "It never worked," he sighed. Down South, gentleman

101 USES FOR KUDZU

#101—Dogcatcher.

1984 Richard Petty drives to his 200th NASCAR victory.

1984 C. Mort Hurst eats 7½ pounds of collards in 30 minutes at the Ayden Collard Festival in North Carolina.

are molded and whipped into shape by strong mamas with little patience for loutishness.

Long ago, in Europe, "gentleman" meant a man of high or noble birth. Social graces and moral rectitude had precious little to do with it. But over here, in the good old democratic USA, the word "gentleman" has never smacked strictly of class or privilege. As boxing champion John L. Sullivan once remarked, "It don't cost nothin' to be a gentleman."

That low price appeals to Southerners. The author of a slim volume offering newcomers tips on life in Winston–Salem notes: "Access to society here involves manners, achievement and breeding. Any two of the three will do." And while you can't choose your parents, or guarantee success in business, manners don't discriminate. Anybody can get himself some.

In Dixie, a gentleman might be rich or poor, black or white, educated or ignorant, but he always abides by a deeply felt code of honor regardless of the cost to himself. He treats others with respect and kindness and puts their wishes above his own. Good upbringing, civility, charm—Southerners deal it in spades from the heart.

Etiquette expert Emily Post defined a gentleman as a man who rises when a lady enters the room. The philospher William James commented that the gentleman remains silent when the vulgarian speaks. And

---

HOW TO
GET ALONG WITH
THE SOUTHERN MAN

Don't invent thoughts for him he's never had.
Don't make fun of him too much.
Always feed him before issuing bad news.
Flatter him shamelessly.
Don't hog the remote control.
Phrase commands as questions.
Send him out to play every now and then.
Pretend to listen.
Ask his opinion and then go on to do whatever you think best.
Let him think it was his idea.

1986   Ernest M. Mickler's *White Trash Cooking* is published.

Ralph Waldo Emerson summed up the gentleman as a man incapable of telling a lie.

Jimmy Carter is one such forthright gentleman. According to Southern lore, just after Carter won the presidency, a Yankee reporter went to Plains to interview Miss Lillian, the new president's mother. Amused and skeptical about all the honesty hype swirling around the president-elect, the reporter smugly asked, "So, Mrs. Carter, is it true that your son has never told a lie?"

"Well," Mrs. Carter responded, "that depends whether you mean a real lie, or just a little old white lie."

Stifling a chuckle at the expense of "rustic Southerners," the smug Yankee rather sarcastically followed up, "Tell me, what exactly would constitute a *'white lie'*?"

Mrs. Carter pondered this for a moment and finally said, "Remember when you got here, I said how happy I was to see you?"

That kind of civility forms the foundation of Southern society. Scholars speculate that the knightly ideal, shooed out of England by Cromwell, took root in the South and bloomed with majestic notions of honor, chivalry, and noblesse oblige. One young Southern Gentleman explained to me how courtesy separates civilization from chaos. "The South is a still a rural place. The farther we are from other people, the more we need rules of civilized behavior," he said. Southerners have good manners for the same reason that the English have tea on the battlefield.

Getting along without manners is like playing a game where you make up the rules as you go along, changing them whenever you feel like it. The Good Old Boy doesn't go gushing all philosophical about it. To

S T E E L   M A G N O L I A S ,
P a r t   O n e

*W*HEN THE LOCAL MEN *were off fighting the Civil War, the ladies of Natchez defended their city without firing a shot. Dressed in their finest clothes and armed with sparkling girlish charms, the Natchez belles descended upon the Yankee officers and began to flirt full force. Once the men in blue had fallen, totally smitten, the belles persuaded them to spare the city.* "Y'all wouldn't be so mean as to burn a girl's very own home down, now would y'all?"

A BRIEF HISTORY OF SOUTHERN MANHOOD, continues

ON CHIVALRY

A New Orleans gentleman: "You pass it on like cancer or heart disease or anything else, it runs in the family, from generation to generation. You don't have much choice about it."

him, good behavior is just part of living a right life. He might not be as polished as the Southern Gentleman, but he knows to open a door, pull out a chair, and help with a wrap. Where the Southern Gentleman strives not to dishonor all those stern ancestors staring down at him from family portraits, the Good Old Boy likely behaves courteously for a more here-and-now reason: "Chicks really love all that politeness crap."

So much so that in Dallas one young entrepreneur capitalized on the demand. He built a business marketing the mystique of the polished Southern Gentleman by leasing himself out to belles as "Beau for the Evening." When a local newspaper ran a story about him, they goofed, but later printed a correction. In the first article, the paper inadvertently noted, "Beau would always be the Southern Gentleman, making every effort to fulfill the needs and desires (expect sex) of his clients." It should have read *"except* sex." You can imagine what wonders that one little typo did for Beau's sales.

These days, even a professional state-of-the-art gent like Beau runs into situations that his mama didn't prepare him for. The modern Southern Gentleman's nightmare dilemma? Whether to hold the door for a preoperative transsexual.

A more conventional question mark arose for a Memphis gentleman not long ago. Entering a downtown office building, he instinctively held open the door for a young woman. Offended, the woman rudely chastised him, yelling "I can open the door for myself, thank you very much!" The gentleman reeled. He apologized, and then spent the rest of the day with the voices of two women echoing in his head: His mama telling him always to hold the door for a lady and the shriek of the incensed feminist telling him to get lost.

"I'm damned if I do, damned if I don't," he said. "Usually I do. I figure if a woman screams at me for being polite, that's her bad manners, not mine."

Most Southern men, young and old, would agree. In Mississippi not long ago, I overheard a twenty-year-old construction worker beg a lady's pardon when he accidentally let slip the word "hell" in her presence. I witnessed another Southern gallant nearing his hundredth birthday stand when two female visitors exited the room; it took nearly five minutes for him to struggle to his feet, but he managed, and the women were charmed.

My neighbor tells a story he believes illustrates the inherent rudeness of Yankees and the natural social superiority of Southerners. "One time a Yankee said right to my face that the heat down here made girls mature fast and get pregnant too young. He also said that it had been scientifically proven that hot weather causes brain damage, and that was why Southerners speak so slowly."

My neighbor felt like punching the Yank's lights out, but as a gentleman, he restrained himself. Instead he matched discourtesy with wit. "The heat may very well cause retardation and early ripening, but apparently the cold of your country causes rudeness."

To the Southerner, rudeness is worse. If the ultra-civilized Dixie boy sees nothing "civil" about the Civil War, you know that the Civil Rights movement bothered him too. But not for the reason you might think. When a fellow values nice manners to a wacko degree, any open social strife pains him. It's sad, but even in hindsight the injustice of segregation bothers the white Southerner not nearly so much as the rudeness of it. To the Southerner—black as well as white—a breach of good behavior remains among the most heinous of crimes. A Dixie boy might forgive bodily injury, but he can never, ever forget hurt feelings or shabby behavior.

One morning when I was in college, I stood brushing my teeth in the upstairs bathroom of the sorority house. Suddenly one of the sisters ran up to me and hurriedly whispered in my ear, "Margie's fixing to ask if you want to be fixed up with her brother this weekend. Trust me—say no."

STEEL MAGNOLIAS,
Part Two

*A*FTER CHARLESTON FELL, *the belles in that city struck at the enemy's nerve center by inviting Yankee military officers to tea. The belles spiked the tea with poisonous oleander leaves that made the soldiers violently ill.*

A BRIEF HISTORY OF SOUTHERN MANHOOD, continues

WHAT'LL IT BE: THE GIRL OR THE BILL OF RIGHTS?

Whenever the Constitution comes between me and the virtues of the women of the South, I say to hell with the Constitution.
—THEODORE BILBO

Quicker than I could rinse, spit, and ask why, she dashed off. Sure enough, a few seconds later in prissed Margie. "Hey, you doing anything this weekend? My brother's in town and he needs a date for the game."

"Sorry, Marge, I've got plans. Some other time."

Later at breakfast, the girl who'd issued the warning gave me the scoop. "He's not bad looking. Good body, smart, and as rich as God, *but —*"

She leaned in close as if she was about to share some national security information, or tell me that Margie's brother was a felon or a dwarf or something. "Girl, it's real, real sad. He was in a car wreck last summer, and *the manners part of his brain was destroyed!* He can't remember a thing about how to be a gentleman."

Margie's brother was a young man stricken in the prime of his gallantry. Medically speaking, I have no idea if there even is such a thing as the etiquette cortex of the human brain. I sort of doubt it. But if such a

GENTLEMAN'S GENTLEMAN

S OUTHERN GENTLEMEN cannot escape their upbringing. Chivalry never takes a vacation. At a large gathering of gay men on a sweltering beach in Miami, a Texas man was approached by a sweaty woman. She said, "Excuse me, but can I wipe my face on your shirt?"

"Oh, no," the man moaned reluctantly. "Are you sure?" he asked, handing her his T-shirt.

Later he explained: "I couldn't help it. When somebody asks for help, you give it. That's just the way I was raised."

1992 Bill Clinton of Arkansas is elected president of the United States. Al Gore of Tennessee is elected vice-president. The University of Alabama wins its twelfth national collegiate football championship.

cell cluster does exist, you can bet it's oversized in the Beulah boy's cranium. If it were possible for a fellow to sustain a blow to his chivalry bits, it would indeed qualify as a catastrophic Southern tragedy. Sad, real sad.

Polish and charm and the considerate nature that gives rise to them combine to make Southern men quality mates and fine friends. Those rascals like women, get the point of women. Even though they'll seldom say so, Southern men usually prefer the company of women. It's not science or anything, but how about this theory as to why Southern men love women with such unusual ardor: They say the Southern belle values her silver so highly because her ancestors almost lost it during the war, right? Well, perhaps that's the reason the Southern beau values woman; he could have lost her during the war. And then where would he be?

Not long ago I met an American woman who'd spent most of her life overseas. She traveled South for a temporary job posting, and noticed the men's politeness almost as soon as she stepped off the airplane. New York City and Los Angeles were the only parts of the United States she'd really experienced before. She half envisioned the lower, right half of the great chasm between Manhat-

**BLOWS
TO
HIS
EGO**

Wife working
Bankruptcy
Son sitting the bench
Empty creel or stringer
Being classified 4-F
Asking directions

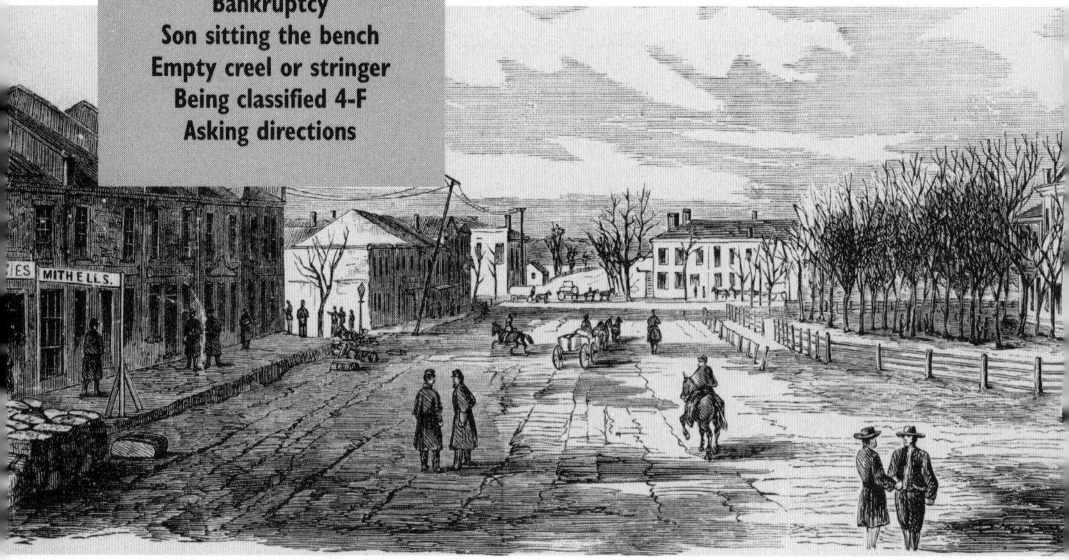

A BRIEF HISTORY OF SOUTHERN MANHOOD, continues

tan and Beverly Hills to be a cultureless wasteland populated with slow-witted bumpkins. She found two pleasant surprises: the food and the menfolk.

"These boys are so well mannered." She marveled at how a dancing partner had allowed her to walk off the dance floor in front of him. "At my office, total strangers hold the door. I mean keep holding it until I walk all the way through! They're so sweet and kind and thoughtful," she gushed. "Are they good lovers? I must try one before I leave. And the catfish too."

A gentleman treats a prince like a laborer and a laborer like a prince. He does not read other people's mail. His handshake is his word. And according to Anita Loos and Southern women everywhere, gentlemen prefer blondes. Southern is as Southern does. Once a gentleman, always a gentleman. A friend from New Orleans keeps this quote stuck to her refrigerator:

> *The true gentleman is the man whose conduct proceeds from good-will and an acute sense of propriety and whose self-control is equal to all emergencies; who does not make the poor man conscious of his poverty, the obscure man conscious of his obscurity, or any man of his inferiority or deformity; who is himself humbled if necessity compels him to humble another; who does not flatter wealth, cringe before power, or boast of his own possessions or achievements; who speaks with frankness, but always with sincerity and sympathy; whose deed follows his word; who thinks of the rights and feelings of others rather than his own; and who appears well in any company. He is a man with whom honor is sacred and virtue is safe.*

This friend lost her husband, a fine Southern Gentleman, last year. She says those words remind her of him and of just how good a good Southern man can be.

1993   Atlanta is announced as the site of the 1996 Olympics.

1994   Charlotte, North Carolina, is awarded an NFL franchise. Memphis, Tennessee, is denied one.
       The movie *Forrest Gump* makes dumb Southern guys hip.

1995   Newt Gingrich of Georgia becomes Speaker of the House of Representatives.

PICTURE CREDITS